THE KNIGHTS OF ABADDON

R. A. BENTON

Cover design courtesy of Christian Beaulieu
Map artwork courtesy of Marisa Pachiarotti

This book is dedicated to:
My mother and father—
For insisting I do my best in school,
My teachers, Alyson and Michael—
For instilling a love for literature,
and
Christian—
For keeping me accountable to my goals.
Lastly,
My wife, Beth—
Your encouragement and support made this possible.

CONTENTS

ACKNOWLEDGMENTS

This book was made possible due in no small part to those already mentioned and for which this book was dedicated.

I would also like to give a special thank you to the folks at Amazon's Createspace publishing department for all the work that has gone into making this book possible.

THE KEEPER'S CHRONICLES

THE BEGINNING

A long time ago (back when time was far more abundant than now), the world was new. Virgin waters ebbed and flowed untouched, grass swayed in a gentle wind, and the sun and the moon danced around the globe, giving light to both day and night. Deer and fawn alike dashed in and out of unending fields of wheat, and the bees flew in clusters betwixt the honeysuckles and the daisies and the lilies and any other flower you might imagine. It's quite hard to explain a place you've never been.

Imagine, if you can, the most beautiful, pristine place you have ever laid eyes upon. Picture this place so vividly that its scent fills the room, the ground is beneath your feet, and the sounds echo in your ears. Can you hear the tumbling water or the rustling leaves amid the summer breeze? Do you smell the fragrance of a million flowers carpeting a valley floor? Whatever place it is you imagine, you can be sure the place in this story is yet more beautiful, more sensational, and more perfect than any other.

The story says that within this place, another place yet more perfect was set aside, grown, and cultivated for a greater purpose. It says that man made an appearance, joined shortly afterward by a woman, and together, they lived in this special place, a place we call The Garden. It was in *this* garden that man and woman lived in *this* world quite peaceably and without fear or danger, death, or disease. As with any good story, the good times do not last. (After all, what good is a happy, nothing-bad-ever-happens kind of story?) In The Garden, two trees were planted at the center. No one knows what these two particular trees looked like, but it has at least been agreed upon that both trees bore some kind of fruit. The man and woman were given very specific instructions not to eat from one of those trees. To do so would have consequences many believe are still with us today. Call it magical properties, call it ethereal attributes, or call it the miraculous, for even those words fail to explain what was so extraordinary about the fruit, the garden, and its inhabitants.

As with any other story, we are hardly surprised that both the man and woman disregarded the ultimate rule. Whether it was for power, greed, self-indulgence, or trickery, the single act of eating the forbidden fruit exiled them both from The Garden. And so it is, to this day, no one has ever set foot in The Garden since.

PROLOGUE: THE ASCENDED KING

Pernic stood in the east wing chambers of Avar Castle, watching black billows overwhelm the fading blue sky. Roaring finger-like flames raged with the ferocity of the cold sea wind, engulfing the city of Ancleed in a single massive fire cloud. Below, he could hear battering rams on the castle doors and the last war cries of a futile effort. The steady cry of an infant child echoed in the royal chambers. He turned away from the large bay windows, his gaze falling to mother and son.

"Milady," said Pernic, dropping to his knees. Queen Nadua looked upon the old sage, her child clutched to her chest. Pernic was dressed in the simplest of robes, colored in earthly tones. Sweat and dirt blended together about his overlarge brows, casting his luminescent green eyes into shadow. Various twigs and leaves rested tangled in his graying and matted hair. His short and untidy beard showed remnants of lingering golden yellow. Across his left cheek, a fresh, thin, and lengthy cut glared in contrast to the many deep wrinkles lining his face. At the floor beside him lay a wooden staff, crooked and heavily worn. When Nadua gave him no reply, Pernic raised his head to gaze upon the queen.

A dark purple cloak concealed most of her ceremonial white gown while not quite hiding the hilt of her sword and the many precious gems embedded within. Long, flowing raven hair hung past her shoulders. Her pale blue eyes glistened with the tears that slid down her pale cheeks. Then without warning, Nadua dropped to her knees, burrowing into Pernic, the infant child now snug between them, and wept. Pernic embraced the queen and her child. His robes quickly became damp with tears.

"He's g-gone, Pernic," the queen sobbed, her voice broken and unsteady.

"I know," said Pernic, his embrace stronger still. "I know." Considerable time passed as Pernic held the queen in the east wing. She was right; the Jarl was undoubtedly gone. Naborus had led his forces past the outer reaches of Ancleed, beyond the rolling hills, to make his stand in the Field of Tears. Ancleed now stood abandoned and ablaze — Naborus had failed. Dedalus had won.

After some time, the queen broke from Pernic's embrace, standing once again, her eyes steady over the city below. She held her son yet closer, as if everything hinged on never letting him go. The child's cries had subsided.

"Milady," said Pernic, now standing beside her, leaning heavily on his staff, "we must get you away from here."

"I cannot leave my people," said Nadua.

"Your people are dead," said Pernic, his voice noticeably unsteady in the moment. It was very unlike him. "Dedalus will be here soon. He will not spare you, and I doubt even I could delay him long."

"What would you have me do?" she asked.

"I beg you, Nadua," said Pernic, "if nothing else but for the child's sake."

"What of Alexander?" she asked. "Surely he will stand against Dedalus."

"The Grand King is dead," answered Pernic. Nadua closed her eyes and breathed heavily.

"I found him and his wife dead in their bed-chambers."

"And their daughter?"

"Safe—for now."

"What of Felix? Surely he was at Alexander's side."

"Nadua, look to the city. White Riders are storming the castle walls this very instant. Felix is either dead, or worse—a traitor." They stood together in silence for a few moments, the battering rams still crashing upon the castle doors below. They would not hold for much longer.

"You're hurt," said Nadua, staring at the cut on Pernic's cheek.

"It is of no concern," replied Pernic.

"Then let me tend to it," said Nadua. She held the babe tightly in one arm, her other outstretched. Pernic gave her a rueful smile while she traced the cut with her fingertips. Her lips moved almost silently, chanting lyrical phrases of an ancient language as she moved back and forth over the cut.

"The wound isn't closing," said Nadua after an intensive minute of tracing the cut.

"I thought as much," said Pernic.

"How did it happen?"

"Another story for another time," said Pernic. "We must leave, Nadua."

"Where can we go, Pernic?"

"To the courtyard," said Pernic. "Eznik and Ilandee will be waiting for us." Nadua gave one last longing look over the city of Ancleed and followed Pernic out the chamber doors. They descended to the main hall, paying no attention to the soldiers who rushed past them toward the castle doors. A guard greeted them at the end of the corridor that led to the west wing courtyard.

"This way, milady," said the guard, pushing the door open. "They haven't yet breached the walls."

"Thank you," said Nadua, following the guard onto the courtyard. The guard led them through the courtyard, his sword drawn and ready. Outside the walls they could hear the deafening sound of battle: the death cries, the tumbling of brick and mortar, and the clash of blade meeting blade. At the end of the courtyard was a grove in the shape of a large circle, a lone standing willow at the center. The guard took to his knee. "We will give you time, milady." Nadua bent toward him and kissed the guard on his exposed cheek. The guard stood, gave a second nod, and returned to the castle.

"Thank heavens you're alive." Pernic and Nadua both turned on their heels. Two figures stepped from the shadows. Ilandee was a towering and broad-shouldered man. His eyes were small and his hair black and neatly trimmed. His face was covered in stubble. He stepped forward and shook Pernic's hand, turning second to Nadua. He did not bow as expected but took her into an embrace.

The second was neither man nor woman. A long and wavy blonde beard covered his chiseled face, and thick, curled horns sprouted from his head. Untamed yellow mane fell past his neck. The hide of his horse body flashed violent streaks of amber. Tattooed on his forehead was an archaic

4

symbol in the shape of a waning crescent moon. On his back, a long bow hung by a strap, and a heavy battle-ax was slung on a belt around his waist.

"Eznik," said Pernic with a quick nod.

"They are moving," said Eznik, his voice very deep and his eyes resting intently on Pernic. "They have left the Field of Tears. They are very near the city."

"Who is moving?" asked Nadua over the staggered cries of her child. She readjusted the covers over the boy.

"The Knights of Abaddon," answered Eznik.

"That's impossible," said Nadua.

"I tell you the truth," said Eznik. "I have seen them with my own eyes."

"But how?" asked Ilandee. "Abaddon has been gone for near a century, and his staff was destroyed."

"If it is a question of skill, Dedalus is more than capable of replicating the cursed artifact," said Pernic.

"What of the sword?" asked Eznik. "Is it safe?"

"That too is in his grasp," answered Pernic sorrowfully, pointing at the slim cut on his cheek. "A failure I will soon regret, undoubtedly."

"But I thought you hid it away," said Nadua.

"I did," said Pernic. "Clearly, not well enough."

"Then you've seen them—the knights?" asked Eznik. Pernic nodded.

"I did not believe my eyes when I saw them descend upon Hoethra. But there is no mistaking it." Eznik gazed into the sky, the first stars emerging in the quickly fading light.

"The stars are hostile tonight," said Eznik.

"There must be something we can do," said Nadua. "Where are the others? Surely we can overpower him with numbers."

"Fayden, Bryan, and Ademus are dead," said Pernic. "I found their bodies in the Room of Knowledge."

"Dedalus," said Nadua through clenched teeth.

"And Ortho, Elwynn, and Goron are missing."

"They've betrayed us too?"

"Perhaps," said Pernic. "It is unwise and unfair to let emotions guide our thoughts to unproven faults."

"So it's over," said Ilandee as he gazed toward Avar Castle. "Everything my brother built — gone." Night had fallen over Ancleed. The castle was breached, and soon escalades would line the outer curtain walls.

"We are out of time," said Pernic. "Ilandee, take Nadua down to the docks —"

"No," said Nadua. Her gaze had turned toward the castle she and her husband had built together. She then looked upon her child in her arms. The babe stared at his mother, suddenly quiet, his eyes bright and blue, like his father's. The hair on his head was also unmistakably his father's — blond and ruffled. She kissed her son gently on the forehead and turned to Ilandee.

"You are his uncle," said Nadua, her eyes wet. "Take him." She held her son for him to take.

"Nadua," said Pernic, his eyes wide and fearful. "Do not be so rash."

"Take him," she said, ignoring Pernic. Ilandee

took the child reluctantly, his expression one of confusion and sadness.

"I do not understand," said Ilandee.

"Just as you were entrusted with Cadmus's son, I will entrust you with mine. They will grow up like brothers. One day you will tell them about their fathers and their mothers." Nadua looked down at her son one last time. From her neck she removed a necklace and placed it around the boy. It was silver, a circular pendent embossed with a tree that resembled that of an oak. She bent low and whispered in his ear and turned from them, running toward the castle, unsheathing her sword. Pernic shouted after her, but she ignored him. A few White Riders emerged onto the courtyard, charging the queen head-on. She raised her blade high, both hands firmly grasping the hilt. With fluid motions, she cut down the advancing Riders, each falling one after the other about the courtyard. Without hesitation, Nadua reentered the castle. Nadua had gone. Pernic turned to Ilandee.

"Go now," said Pernic. "I will be in contact with you soon. Clifford is waiting for you at the docks with a ship—hurry." Ilandee nodded to both of them in turn, and with his nephew held firmly in his arms, he dashed into the shadows and was quickly out of sight.

"We shall meet again, Pernic of Edel," said Eznik, "when the boys are grown."

"Haste to your safety, Eznik of Ragnar." Eznik reared on his hind legs and galloped after Ilandee, leaving Pernic alone in the courtyard. More White Riders advanced into the courtyard, coming from the castle and over the curtain walls. Pernic raised his staff and looked toward the sky. Light emanated from Pernic, white and immeasurably bright, filling the night sky with its intense glow and the sound of thunder. When the light had faded, Pernic was gone and the Riders were facedown on the hard stone of the courtyard. A heavy rain fell over Ancleed, and the raging fires quenched.

With the final hammer stroke of the battle at Ancleed, Dedalus returned to Hoethra and seized the empty Grand Throne. His ascendency tossed Aldure into a slow-spreading darkness and would split the land in two, brewing civil war between the east and west. Murder and thievery became commonplace throughout the land as the Band of Kings was abolished and the Magistrate forever replaced by a single commune of handpicked corrupt officials soon to be known as the Imperium. The White Riders forever abandoned their honor-bound duty as peacekeepers under the late Grand King Alexander, fundamentally transforming themselves into a private military organization led by Knight Commander Felix Alric, who pledged loyalty to the new Grand King; Dedalus.

With dwindled numbers and multiple betrayals of their own, Pernic called a permanent recess on the Council of Sages and fled from the public eye, never to be seen or heard from again. The Imperium, with the Grand King's authority, forbade the practice and tenets of the Old Way. Those who refused were punished by death.

Sixteen years later, relentless freezing rain tore the remaining scarlet maple leaves from weak branches as the autumn season fell. Fallen tamarack needles covered the root-infested ground in a dull gold carpet as a light but frigid wind blew between the bare tamaracks, carrying the aroma of wet grass through the Sigrún Wilds. Overlooking Hoethra's Imperial Highway, two young men sat expectantly patient on a low-rising ridge surrounded by oppressive year-round fog, involuntary victims of Aldure's cruel elements.

CHAPTER ONE: CHILDREN NO MORE

Dagon!" he shouted, holding high a smooth oval stone in his right hand. "I bet I can skip t his rock more times than you!" Tagorin walked to the edge of the mirror-surface lake, glancing momentarily at his swimming reflection. A young boy with short ruffled blond hair and a dirt-smudged face grinned back at him.

"You wish," said a second boy striding up beside, making an appearance in the reflection next to Tagorin. Dagon swept away the curtain of black hair covering his face, revealing stone-gray eyes that disappeared into the lake's surface.

"OK, here it goes," said Tagorin, launching the smooth skipping stone into the lake. The stone repelled off the gray water, sending a cascade of ripples from the place of impact. Two, three, four, five, six times the oval stone hit the water, each sending a rally of ripples colliding into the other before the stone sunk on the seventh splash. Tagorin grinned at Dagon, confident.

"You always lose," said Dagon, plunging his hand into the icy water. "What makes you think you will win this time?" A moment later, Dagon withdrew his hand (now slightly red), pulling with it a perfect circular stone.

"That's my best yet," replied Tagorin. "Your best is six."

Dagon rose to full height and staggered his feet. He gripped the stone with his left thumb and forefinger and arched his back as his arm retracted to full capacity. Dagon held this position for a few seconds, as if he were painted into the surrounding landscape, and then hurled the stone. One, two, three, four, five, six, seven, eight, nine, ten…

"Looks like ten is my new best," said Dagon, giving Tagorin a sideways glance with a broad, tooth-revealing smile.

"Two out of three," said Tagorin as he scoured the shore for another stone.

"I will always be tougher than you, Tagorin…"

"Wake up, Tagorin," whispered Dagon as he tapped Tagorin's shoulder. Groaning, Tagorin opened his eyes. Heavy rain descended upon them now.

"How long was I out?" asked Tagorin, looking up at Dagon as he shook away the excess water gathered on his rain-soaked cloak. Steady raindrops ran down his curtain hair.

"An hour at least," scolded Dagon. Tagorin cowered into the base of the leaning tamarack, attempting to hide from Dagon's accusing stone-gray eyes.

"So-sorry, Dagon, I didn't—"

"You're always sorry."

"I—"

"Forget it," said Dagon waving his hand dismissively. "Now, get up—the caravan will be along any moment." Without word, Tagorin picked up his bow and quiver beside him and followed Dagon silently to the edge of the ridge. Vast, scattered puddles had formed in the deeply worn wagon-wheel grooves of the Imperial Highway while thick, low-lying fog made it nearly impossible to see beyond twenty yards in either direction.

"You remember the plan?" asked Dagon.

"I th-think so," replied Tagorin, setting down his bow and quiver beside him. Dagon shook his

11

head.

"Are you cold, little boy?"

"I'm n-not a little boy."

"You had me fooled," said Dagon wryly.

"Shut it!" Tagorin hissed. He glared at Dagon as he wrapped the cloak tighter around his torso.

"That's better," mocked Dagon. "But I wonder how you intend to use that bow when you're bundled up like a baby."

"I said sh-shut it!"

"I'm going to explain the plan again, so listen this time," said Dagon, ignoring Tagorin.

"I do listen."

"Our job," continued Dagon as though he hadn't heard Tagorin, "is to take out any accompanying White Riders." Tagorin nodded.

"Tiber and his men will be responsible for the actual caravan," said Dagon. Tagorin nodded a second time.

"The information we have says the caravan is made up of an imperial stagecoach bringing essential supplies from Avlōvan to the capital. Accompanying the stagecoach are six White Riders. We have to take them out before the stagecoach reaches Tiber and his men."

"Got it."

"I hope so," said Dagon, his eyes darting from one side to the other. "This fog is going to make it difficult. We have a short window in which to operate."

"You wo-worry to-too much, Dagon," said Tagorin. "You—"

Dagon rapidly held up his hand to silence Tagorin.

"Wh-what's the matter?"

"Shh," replied Dagon, now listening intently. And then Tagorin heard it: hooves. The caravan approached. "Quick, get down and ready your bow."

Tagorin hastily picked up his bow and moved down the ridge, placing a three-arms'-length distance between himself and Dagon.

"Don't forget your arrows, idiot," said Dagon, pointing to the quiver Tagorin had left near an un-earthed and protruding root. Tagorin stumbled to his sleeping tree. Snatching the shoulder strap with one hand, he again turned toward the ridge edge, tripping over the bulging root. The quiver, grasped loosely in his hand, flew from his grip and fell the fifty feet to the base of the ridge.

"You idiot, Tagorin!" gasped Dagon.

"I'm sorry," whispered Tagorin.

"Curses." Dagon tossed his quiver between them and quickly divided out the arrows as the hooves of the caravan horses approached.

"Here," said Dagon, tossing three arrows at Tagorin's feet and leaving three for himself. "Pray to the gods we don't miss one." Tagorin stared at the arrows thrown at his feet.

"Here they come," said Dagon as he notched his first arrow and drew back on the string. Uncontrollable shakes began passing through Tagorin's body, starting with his hands.

"Get a hold of yourself!" urged Dagon. "I can't take them all out by myself." Tagorin attempted to notch an arrow, but the severe shaking in his hands forced him to drop it.

"Hurry," said Dagon, "they are almost in

sight." On a second attempt, Tagorin notched the arrow, but the shaking in his limbs made it difficult to steady his aim.

"On my count," whispered Dagon. "One…"

I can't miss.

"Two…" The shadowy figures were now present within the fog, and the thunder of hooves boomed over the heavy frozen rain.

"Three!" Dagon yelled as two White Riders burst through the fog. Dagon released the bowstring, launching the arrow toward the closest Rider. Blood spattered onto the Rider's white silk garments as he fell backward off his rearing white stallion. Not wanting to be outdone, Tagorin let loose his own arrow, sending it into the neck of the remaining Rider in the front. The Rider fell like his comrade, landing face-first on the muddy highway while his stallion reared and fled into the forest.

"Archers!" shouted the driver of the five-team Percheron-driven stagecoach. Tagorin notched his second arrow and aimed for the lead horse of the caravan.

"Never mind the horses," shouted Dagon as he sent his second arrow flying. "Take out the Riders. Tiber's men will take care of the caravan." Three Riders remained.

"Hurry, now," encouraged Dagon as he released his last arrow while Tagorin launched his second. Both arrows met their targets.

"Hurry, Tagorin," Dagon shouted, brandishing his bow uselessly. Tagorin breathed slowly and notched his last arrow. His stomach throbbed constantly now, but his earlier shakes had subsided from the excitement of the hunt. The caravan was no longer in sight, and the last Rider was nearing the extent of his vision.

"Tagorin, he's nearly gone!" Dagon shouted again, eyes wide and fearful. Tagorin gave one last extra tug and released the last arrow they had just as the Rider vanished into the fog. Silence followed, then, a soft splash accompanied by the bray of a stallion. Dagon did not wait for Tagorin; he leaped from his kneeling position and took off along the ridge and in the direction of the fleeing Rider. Tagorin took another deep breath and followed.

Thirty yards up the ridge, Tagorin found Dagon peering down at the sixth White Rider, facedown in a large puddle nearly equal his size with an arrow protruding straight up in his back. The Rider's silk white garments soaked up the blood like a sponge. His horse was nowhere to be found.

"That was too close," said Dagon, short of breath.

"I ca-can't believe we're that lucky," replied Tagorin, his teeth chattering again with the renewed awareness of the piercing cold rain hammering down on them.

"Humph," answered Dagon. "We wouldn't have had to be lucky if not for that mishap of yours. You seem to have them frequently."

"Not on pur-purpose."

"We should head up the road," said Dagon, ignoring Tagorin's discomfort. "Tiber will be waiting." They stayed on the ridge, eyes peeled for the halted stagecoach, with any luck held enough supplies to make it through the fast-approaching winter.

Ten minutes later and where the ridge descended to ground level, they found the caravan toppled over and lying on its side. Two of the five Percherons lay dead on the road while one of Tiber's men readied a branding rod to alter the Imperial seal found on all Imperial horses. Most of the men, however, huddled over various crates while a few men began loading down the newly acquired and soon-to-be brand-altered Percherons.

"'Urry it up," yelled a thundering voice. Tiber stood at the edge of the road holding an old tobacco pipe while barking commands to the men. His brown burly beard covered most of his face while his shoulder-length hair was tied into a ponytail. Beneath his unfastened cloak, a leather strap sheathing half a dozen knives ran across his body. His tiny hazel eyes lit up slightly as the two young men approached.

"Well, looky here," boomed Tiber. "Ilandee's li'tle heroes."

"We do our best," replied Dagon smartly.

"Humph," snorted Tiber. "Still a bunch o' kids to me."

"So our part is done, right?" asked Dagon.

"Yeah, you two can 'ead on back to camp. Everythin's taken care o' here."

"Let's go, Tagorin," said Dagon.

"S-see you later, Tiber," said Tagorin, wrapping his cloak ever more tightly.

On the return journey along the Imperial Highway, Dagon stopped and picked up Tagorin's fallen quiver and haphazardly shoved it into Tagorin's chest.

"Try not to lose this next time."

"I d-didn't lose it."

"May as well have," replied Dagon. Tagorin didn't respond.

"Let's go home," said Dagon, shaking his head.

Home was a camp situated near the southern shore side of Lake Gray, nestled neatly between two moderately high-rising hills that shielded them from the worst of Aldure's harsh winter winds. Every now and then, the company would be forced to uproot itself and find a temporary place to lay low when scouting parties were sent to find the "barbarians" they had come to be known as. Regardless of this, however, the company always found itself returning to the same place. Lake Gray itself was not very large, but it was immeasurably deep, and strewn along most of its shoreline were large and round water-polished stones, accompanied by less abundant smaller counterparts, perfect for skipping. Lake Gray had earned its name due in part to the surface of the water, always a slate gray that gradually blurred into the mist until both were indistinguishable from the other; nature's mirror. Tamaracks and pines lined the rocky shore, their feeble roots exposed from the long-washed-away soil.

It did not take very long for the two young men to reach the southern shore of Lake Gray from the edge of the Imperial Highway. The icy rain had subsided, and the wind momentarily calmed. Tagorin took a familiar seat up on a smooth boulder half on the shore and half-submerged in the lake, removing his bow and quiver while Dagon leaned against one of the frail tamaracks, keeping his distance from the shore. Tagorin lay on his back, staring into the slate sky.

Shrugging, Tagorin leaned over to one side of the boulder, sifting through the various shore sediments until he found a smooth polished rock, perfect for skipping. A small grin formed on his face. He leaped from the boulder and stood, legs apart, facing the lake.

"Hey, Dagon," said Tagorin. "I bet I can skip this rock more times than you." Dagon snorted but turned his head to watch Tagorin launch the smooth skipping stone into the water. The stone rebounded off the water, sending a massive ripple upon impact. Two, three, four, five, six, seven, eight, nine, ten times the polished stone hit the water, each contact sending a rally of ripples before the stone sank on the eleventh splash. Tagorin looked over his shoulder to Dagon, who hadn't budged.

"Your turn," said Tagorin. Dagon shook his head.

"No thanks."

"Come on," Tagorin pleaded. "I'll even find the stone for you."

"We're not children anymore," said Dagon, abandoning his leaning post. He turned his back to Tagorin, walking away from the shore and back into the misted forest. "We'd best be going, or they'll be sending search parties for our bodies."

They walked without a single word between each other for nearly an hour as daylight faded and the trail grew wider and more worn. The tamaracks grew more spread apart and the fog lessened a little while the growing and flickering spots of orange and yellow at the base of a hill came into view.

Hundreds of small brown and gray tents dotted the clearing. A large fire burned in the center, where a lone, beefy man tended a cauldron with a large wooden spoon clasped in his hands. Tiny torches were scattered on makeshift poles, where shadowy silhouettes of men and women sitting outside their tents could be seen. Others were huddled together conversing softly. By the time they walked into camp, a starless night had fallen on them.

"Well, well," said a towering man who had been waiting to greet them. A broad smile hidden behind a bushy, gray-streaked black beard beamed down on them. "Looks like the last of our children have finally grown into men."

CHAPTER TWO: INHERITANCE

Well, don't just stare at me," encouraged Ilandee, gazing down at the two young men lost for words. His soft amber eyes glistened with pride. "Word was sent ahead of you; you performed marvelously."

"We—we did our best," said Dagon, finding words. Ilandee laughed, stepping between the two young men and placing an arm around each of their shoulders, walking them into the camp.

"Took your time returning, I might add," continued Ilandee, jostling through the camp.

"We had a bit of a hold-up," replied Dagon, glancing at Tagorin.

"What's that supposed to mean?" asked Tagorin.

"You insisted we stop at the lake," said Dagon.

"I just wanted to toss a few stones is all," said Tagorin.

"You're not a child anymore."

"Now, now, Dagon," Ilandee interrupted. "Even I enjoy a little relaxation from time to time." He glanced at Tagorin, giving him a wink. "Come to think of it, I haven't tossed stones in years."

"Let's go tomorrow," insisted Tagorin.

"Sounds like a splendid idea," replied Ilandee.

"Sometimes, I think I'm the only adult around here," murmured Dagon. Ilandee laughed again.

"That might well be," joked Ilandee. "But enough of this for now. Let's get some grub." The three of them made their way to the center of camp.

"Supper ready, Gregory?" asked Ilandee.

"'Bout as ready as she'll get, I'm afraid," replied the stout man behind the cooking cauldron as he made three more rotations around the boiling stew with the wood-whittled spoon he still gripped in both hands. A burly mustache quivered as he spoke. "All we 'ave left is meat an' carrots."

"At least we have salt," said Ilandee, eyeing the stew.

"'Fraid not," said Gregory. "An' before anybody asks, we're outta pepper too."

"Well," said Ilandee with a crooked smile while picking up a tin bowl, "bottom's up." One by one, Gregory ladled the stew into their bowls while the rest of the camp quickly filed in line.

"Tiber and his crew are running a little behind, it seems," said Ilandee, taking a seat around the center fire pit. "They are going to be disappointed to miss this treat of a meal."

"Not too disappointed," murmured Dagon as he lifted a spoonful, only to tip his spoon to watch a single chunk of meat splash into the carrot broth. Gradually, the noise around the fire grew as more of the company congregated for supper. Nearly every supper was filled with the same drudgery; imperial news, rumors of rebellion in towns Tagorin had never visited, and the occasional sightings of demon knights traveling through the mountain corridors where no one dared adventure any longer.

"Did you hear what happened over in Finoval?" asked a man with a cane who sat across from Ilandee. The man was slightly hunched over from years of hard labor, his right arm hanging at a very odd angle. His short silver hair receded near

21

to the crown of his head. His name was Clifford, but nearly everyone affectionately called him Vine.

"The new Overseer?" Ilandee suggested.

"Indeed," said Vine, jerking his cane in such a fashion he dropped his stew to the ground. The man merely shrugged his shoulders and went on. "Finoval has become the headquarters of that traitorous scum commander Felix Alric and his White Rider gang." This brought a few angry cries from others in the company.

"I have heard the rumor," said Ilandee.

"Well, it isn't a rumor," encouraged Vine. "See for yourself." Vine struggled momentarily to reach into the satchel beside him. A moment of shuffling later Vine handed Ilandee a crumpled post flier. Ilandee quickly scanned the leaflet then, clearing his throat, began reading aloud the post:

In a daring move, his royal majesty nominated long-standing serviceman Felix Alric to fill the empty post of Finoval's Overseer during last week's Imperium session. Felix Alric, commander of the White Rider Order since its foundation, will now take on an additional leadership role. Felix Alric served as commander of the White Rider Order during the reign of King Alexander, his royal majesty's worthy predecessor. Many suspect for the first time since its creation, the White Rider Order will relocate to Finoval, abandoning its traditional housing in the Imperial Capital of Hoethra so that Felix can maintain both responsibilities with more ease. No official comments have addressed this concern.

Ilandee returned the flier to Vine.

"You know what this means," said Vine. "It

22

means we have to switch targets."

"I will consider it," replied Ilandee.

"Consider it? What's to consider? We can't go marching into Finoval with Alric and the entire order ready to clap us in chains."

"I said I will consider it," replied Ilandee again, this time with sharpness previously absent.

"My apologies," said Vine, bowing his head. His body shook as he attempted to retrieve the tin bowl at his feet. Ilandee retrieved it for him. Vine offered a second nod and went to Gregory without another word. Ilandee peered into his stew for a moment as if searching for answers hidden in his bowl.

Night had arrived, and with it a deafening silence among the camp. Brief whispers traveled through the men, all issuing concern for a plan Tagorin had never heard. Just as Tagorin was gathering the courage to ask Ilandee about this unknown plan, Tiber and the retrieving party arrived. The men stood and applauded; hope had arrived in the form of stolen steeds, recently harvested vegetables, a modest strongbox of tax collections, freshly tailored silks for royalty, a small assortment of spices (chiefly among them salt), and the essential barrels of mead—everything essential and everything exceedingly rare in Aldure. Ilandee was the first to greet Tiber. Without delay, Tiber handed him a parcel of parchment. Ilandee carefully considered the list.

"Everything is accounted for?" asked Ilandee.

"Yep," replied Tiber. "Four barrels o' mead, two barrels o' apple cider, three healthy horses with the brandin' already altered, seven bushels o' carrots, two bushels o' corn, an' one bushel o' grain fer the horses. Two small crates o' silk dresses—might fetch us a good price—a crate each o' gloves an' fur pellets, two pounds each o' salt an' pepper, an' a pound of stuff I've never seen. All that's left is the money box."

"Good work," said Ilandee, surveying the burdened horses. "Unload the horses; we can distribute essentials in the morning." Tiber nodded, pointed at a few of his men (all of whom grunted in unison), and followed Ilandee toward the stew cauldron and the boys.

"Time for bed," said Ilandee, looking down at the two of them.

"We are adults too, you know," insisted Dagon, who had been silent through the whole ordeal.

"Stay up, then," replied Ilandee. "Tomorrow will come early, and the adults have great work to accomplish."

"Good night," Dagon replied, dropping his empty bowl to the ground and setting off toward his tent.

"You should follow his lead, Tagorin." Ilandee gave him a flicker of a smile.

"Are we going to Finoval?" asked Tagorin. Ilandee gave him a hard look.

"We'll talk tomorrow." Tagorin knew not to press the issue—he knew well enough Ilandee's dismissive tone. His tent was not far from the cook's cauldron. Often, he would sit awake, catching bits and fragments of news often kept from the ears of children. This sometimes led to stern lectures from both Ilandee and Tiber. They kept the whole thing together, just the two of them.

Gradually, the fires of the camp diminished and tent-side lanterns were blown out. Silence fell on the camp as complete darkness descended, absent the moon and stars.

It wasn't a mysterious noise that woke Tagorin—it had been the complete silence. It wasn't unusual for him to wake in the dead of the night, often, for the same reason as now. Tagorin shuffled a bit in his blanket, fluffed his flattened pillow, and tried again.

"So it's true." Ilandee's voice floated through the flap of Tagorin's tent.

"No mistakin' it," affirmed Tiber. Silence fell. Then: "We can't change targets. It'd take too long to move in the firs' place, an' we'd use up all our rations we jus' got today."

"I don't plan to change targets," said Ilandee.

"It'd be downright tough to get into Finoval with Alric prancin' around an' all. It's well an' good he forgets my face—but yours, well, you and 'im go way back. He sees you an' we're done." Silence again.

"I know," said Ilandee after a minute had passed. "Let's think on it in the morning—perhaps the answer will come in a dream."

Morning arrived quickly for Tagorin; sleep had evaded him throughout the night. Much of the camp was alive and bustling, gathered in a large circle around the crates and barrels from yesterday's harvest. The morning fog lay low at the outskirts of the camp. He could hear Tiber's voice calling names one by one as the goods were divided among the guild. Worried of losing his hard-earned share, Tagorin hastily doused his face with cold water from the canteen beside his bedroll and rushed to join the other men.

"Tagorin, hurry it up," called Dagon, who stood at the perimeter of the gathered men.

"Why didn't you wake me?" asked Tagorin.

"I'm not your keeper," said Dagon.

"What's the share?"

"Each person gets two pints of honey mead, one pair of gloves, a single fur pellet, and seven silvers," answered Dagon.

"What are you planning to buy?" Tagorin asked. Dagon only shrugged as his name floated through the crowd. Dagon waved and inserted himself into the crowd, disappearing a moment later. A minute passed before Tagorin heard his own name.

"Excuse me," said Tagorin, trying to slip past two of the men in front of him. He tried forcing himself between them, but they wouldn't budge. Frustrated, Tagorin moved along the perimeter and tried again between two other men. Again, no one budged. Tiber called his name a second time. Panicked, Tagorin took a few steps backward and tried a running start. He hit one of the men straight on, but instead of pushing through, Tagorin was launched backward and fell flat on his back. The man blocking the way looked over his shoulder, giving Tagorin a quick look.

"Watch where you're going, runt." Then, not a moment later, Tagorin heard a soft chuckle behind him. Ilandee stood over him with a smile on his face. He reached down and grasped Tagorin by the forearms and lifted, pulling Tagorin up with such force he was temporarily airborne.

"You need to be tougher with this lot," said Ilandee, chuckling while he dusted the dirt from Tagorin's clothes.

"They're bigger than me," argued Tagorin.

"What of it?" replied Ilandee, placing a hand on Tagorin's shoulder.

"Stand aside," Ilandee bellowed, guiding Tagorin into the crowd as it parted in waves to let them through.

"You see, Tagorin?" said Ilandee. "All you need is a good, hearty voice."

"Easy for you to say," said Tagorin. "You run this lot." Ilandee gave him a quick smirk. Dagon stood next to a very irritated Tiber, who was holding a long role of parchment.

"What kept you?" asked Dagon.

"No one let me pass," said Tagorin. "How'd you get through so easily?"

"I'm tough."

"You're not that tough."

"I'll always be tougher than you, Tagorin."

"I 'ate to break up your little chat, but there are others waitin'," growled Tiber. He shoved a small satchel into Tagorin's chest and rushed him away from the center.

"Relax, Tiber," said Ilandee, still smiling. He placed a hand on both their shoulders and led them away from Tiber's lecture concerning relaxation — none of which were pleasant.

"On second thought," said Ilandee, as the three of them were halfway through the crowd, "why don't you stay and help Tiber, Dagon."

"Why?"

"Well, I have a task that needs attending, and one of you will suffice well enough," said Ilandee. "Besides, weren't you saying yesterday that you were the only adult here? Dividing out the shares is a very important adult task."

"And you'll be doing?"

"Tagorin and I will be doing a much less important task, far below your level of expertise. Your talents would be quite wasted."

"Why do I get the feeling you aren't doing anything at all?"

"I have no idea what you are talking about," dismissed Ilandee. "Run along now." Dagon shrugged, muttered a few inaudible words, and made his way back to Tiber.

"Come along, Tagorin," said Ilandee, leading them out of the camp.

"Where are we going?" asked Tagorin.

"I will explain along the way," said Ilandee.

They walked well into the late morning along the very same path Dagon and Tagorin had returned home on the night before. The fog grew increasingly thick as they left the clearing long behind.

"I thought we'd use the opportunity to toss some stones," said Ilandee at last.

"Really?"

"Sure," said Ilandee. "It's been a while since I took you or Dagon to the lake."

"Why did you leave Dagon behind, then?"

"Unfortunately, this world has made him grow up," said Ilandee. "And soon, you will have no choice but to do the same, I'm afraid."

"But I am grown up," argued Tagorin. Ilandee chuckled.

"It wasn't intended to rile you up," assured Ilandee. "Being grown up isn't at all the glamour you perceive."

Noon approached as Lake Gray emerged from behind the fog. Tagorin immediately combed the shoreline, turning over large stones in the search for smaller relatives.

"That one won't do," said Ilandee, gazing at Tagorin's first pick. Water-polished, oval in shape, not too thick, not too thin, and almost crimson and dotted with specs of silver—the stone's perfection glinted in Tagorin's eyes.

"It's perfect," insisted Tagorin.

"No, it's a ways off perfect," said Ilandee, holding out his own selection for Tagorin to see; like his own, Ilandee's stone had been crafted flawlessly by Lake Gray's wind waves, only a miniscule thicker than an eighth of an inch, and oval in shape. At first glance, the only difference between the stones was color. Ilandee's stone matched his own eyes—pure amber and without blotches of any kind.

"I don't see the difference," said Tagorin. In weight, shape, and thickness, they were almost exact—twins.

"Let's test them, then, shall we?"

Tagorin tossed his first; he pulled his throwing arm back, slowly and deliberately—no wasted movement. He kept his eyes locked on the spot where his stone would make first contact. Then, with all the force his right arm could channel, he hurled the stone toward the lake.

The stone hit the lake with a soft splash and floated back into the air. The ripples were large and rapid, distorting the tamaracks' many reflections. One, two, three, four, five, six, seven, eight, nine, ten, eleven times the stone crashed the surface of Lake Gray, sinking below the surface of the mirror lake on the twelfth splash.

"Not bad," Ilandee commended. "It will be tough to beat."

"Don't worry if you don't," said Tagorin, who couldn't contain his smile. "I will give you another chance."

"I'm grateful," replied Ilandee as he approached the shoreline, the edge of the water just barely touching the tips of his boots. He held the stone gently with both hands slightly quivering. The veins in his hands were heavily protruding, and his knuckles were red and thickly lined with rough skin. With his left hand he slowly adjusted the stone to sit purposefully between his right thumb and point finger. He went on in that fashion for minutes it seemed to Tagorin, who didn't mind—Ilandee was thrice his age.

"Are you ready?" Ilandee asked as his arm slowly arched back.

"I was going to ask you the same," answered Tagorin. Ilandee chuckled and launched his stone into the lake. The stone flew as if wings were attached; it skimmed the surface of the lake on its first touch, gliding back into the air and leaving only the smallest ripple. Each time, the stone would touch gently and return to air as if by choice, fighting the rules of the universe. On the seventh touchdown, the stone had not yet lost any momentum, its strides equal to the previous ones. Tagorin, having taken his favorite seat, now stood at the edge of the half-submerged boulder, watching the stone's miraculous flight—ten, eleven, twelve, thirteen, fourteen, fifteen—

Ilandee laughed as the stone finally plummeted on the sixteenth splash.

"Two out of three," said Tagorin, leaping from the boulder.

"All right, but I have something I want to give you first." Ilandee sat down on one of the large boulders inland, crammed between two leaning tamaracks.

"What is it?" asked Tagorin. He rarely received anything from Ilandee—he could recall each item perfectly. The first had been a pocketknife, his first one. The second had been a bow—the one he still used. He did not know what to expect this time— perhaps a sword (like the one Tiber almost always wore at his side) or a new sharpening stone, as some of the guildsmen had mentioned.

"I've held on to this for a long time," said Ilandee. He reached into his cloak and withdrew a small leather pouch with a drawstring. "I think now is the time to return it to you."

"I don't understand," said Tagorin.

"Well, it does require a good bit of explaining, doesn't it?" Ilandee went on. "I told you some time ago that I found you in a village that had appeared to be abandoned — you weren't yet a year old by the looks of you."

"I remember," said Tagorin.

"Well, your story isn't much different from many back at the camp, mine included," continued Ilandee. "Many of us are without our birth families, abandoned in one sense or the other, choice or not. It's what brought us all together, I think, more than anything else."

"You've told me this before," said Tagorin, anxious again for the content hidden in the pouch in Ilandee's hand.

"Yes, of course," said Ilandee, waving his free hand dismissively. "It's the habit of old age; we have to remind ourselves the beginning to properly reach the end." Tagorin could make neither heads nor tails of this but nodded in agreement anyway.

"As I was saying," said Ilandee, loosening the drawstrings of the pouch, "when I discovered you, I found you wearing this." He held the pouch up, gesturing for Tagorin to hold out his hands. Then, delicately, Ilandee dumped the contents of the pouch into Tagorin's hands; a silver chain dropped with a soft clink.

The necklace was almost weightless in his hands. Ilandee had kept it near perfect; the silver of the chain glinted bright, the large tree split in two (most resembling an oak) was well embossed in the center on both sides, and the miniscule runes around the edge of the circular frame were still legible, though Tagorin could not read them:

ᚱᛖᚷᚹᛖᚷ

"You kept this?" asked Tagorin, still eyeing the necklace with surprise. "It must have been worth something." He looked at Ilandee, who replied only with a large smile that distorted the wrinkles around his eyes.

"It most certainly is," said Ilandee after a moment. "But it was not mine to barter, and nor should you be tempted to do likewise. It is a beautiful necklace, and above all, I would imagine, a gift that is not without a purpose." Tagorin smiled. He took the necklace and clasped it around his neck.

"It belonged to them," said Tagorin, finally. Ilandee nodded.

"It surely did."

Tagorin looked out again toward the lake and remembered another promise. He stood up, went to the shoreline for the second time, and scoured for his next stone. When he found one, he held it up so Ilandee could see.

"Two out of three, remember?"

Ilandee laughed as he too walked over to the shore to examine Tagorin's stone.

"That one won't do either."

CHAPTER THREE: BREAKING CAMP

That night prior to supper, Ilandee summoned all the guildsmen to assemble. Whispers broke out, spreading from one huddled cluster to another while the women (far less in number than the men) pretended to busy themselves with to-do lists. Gregory attended the cauldron halfheartedly, his eyes glued to Ilandee while he stirred the pot with well-practiced precision.

"As many of you are aware," said Ilandee, pacing in front of the waiting stew, "our plan to infiltrate Finoval has grown complex. Initially, we—"

"We're walking straight to the gallows," shouted Vine. Many of the men shouted in agreement.

"He's right," insisted the bald one sitting next to Vine. "The place'll be burstin' at the seams with White Riders."

"We should just stay here," said Vine. "We have plenty to see us through for a while."

"Quiet," Ilandee asserted, raising his hands high. He waited until the scattered debates subsided before continuing. "We have made changes to the plan. Initially, we had planned to infiltrate Finoval as traders and attack from within during nightfall. Obviously, with the White Rider Order relocated to Finoval, we cannot proceed as planned. We will split into two teams—one led by Tiber and the other by yours truly. We will then enter Finoval as traders, unload our acquired goods to the local markets, and leave without further incident. We will need to be fast and efficient.

"Our relocation site is to be located about ten miles from Finoval, well away from the city, at the base of the Hackastine Mountains. We'll gain access not only to Finoval's markets, but also the constant sea trade.

"For those of you who are new with us—familiarize yourselves with the proper procedures. We operate in partners—*always*. Those of you with little or no experience have been paired with someone more seasoned. When I call your names, introduce yourselves if you don't already know each other and review the procedures. Those of you who did not receive clearance to participate will be responsible for moving camp materials to the disclosed relocation site. Speak with Gregory if you have questions. We break camp at sunrise. Eat well and rest—we have a long journey tomorrow." Then, to everyone's displeasure, Ilandee pulled from the insides of his cloak a tightly rolled parchment scroll and let it loose. The scroll fell open, unraveling nearly the length of Ilandee's entire body. One by one, the names of all the guildsmen participating in the approaching raid were called and paired.

Nearly an hour passed as Ilandee assigned pairs, each taking longer than the previous. Some men had questions regarding shares, others disagreed with the pairings, and some felt it necessary to mention concerns they had as to the guild's ultimate goal—to all of which Ilandee irritably gave short answers. Then, at last, Ilandee made his way through the crowd and took a seat next to Tagorin and Dagon.

"And that leaves you two," said Ilandee,

slightly short of breath.

"So we're working together, right?" asked Tagorin.

"You never did pay attention very well," Ilandee asserted. "Neither you nor Dagon have gone on an outing such as this. You, like everyone else, have been paired with a more experienced guildsman." Both Dagon and Tagorin looked around; all the guildsmen and women stood in line waiting for supper, chatting idly away.

"Who then?" asked Dagon.

"Well," said Ilandee, "Dagon, you have been assigned to go with Tiber." Ilandee pointed off in the direction toward the storage tent where Tiber stood just outside, routinely checking the camp's inventory. Dagon stood, nodded without a word, and marched toward the storage tent. While Dagon hid his excitement, Tagorin knew he couldn't have been happier with the decision. Dagon had always taken a liking to Tiber (though Dagon never explained why). The well-known fact that Dagon rarely confided in anyone left much about him unanswered.

"Which leaves you with me," said Ilandee as he cast a small grin at Tagorin. "I trust you're not too disappointed."

"Not at all," replied Tagorin. "But I had hoped Dagon and I could go together."

"One day, perhaps you shall."

"What is Finoval like?"

"Well," answered Ilandee, "it's not like the villages you've visited before. Finoval is a city, one of the twelve cities of the Old Kingdom—easy to lose yourself in and full of bizarre people. But its best experienced rather than explained."

"Are there a lot of things to buy?"

"More than you could ever hope to purchase," said Ilandee. "Unfortunately, we won't have time for that—I'm afraid Felix doesn't like us much, and extending our stay longer than necessary would prove detrimental."

"You know him, right?" Ilandee glared at Tagorin.

"I should do better to avoid your tent at night," replied Ilandee.

"Well?"

"Yes," Ilandee admitted, rising to a stand. "But that is a story for another time. It's late, and we all have a long journey ahead. Get some food and call it a night." He gave a quick grin and shuffled toward his own tent. Tagorin followed his orders; he quickly downed the stew (an improvement to the night prior) and made the short journey to his tent. Beside him, Dagon's tent-side lantern had been blown out.

He must already be asleep.

Tagorin blew out his own lantern, crawled into the tent, and settled into his bedroll.

Tagorin crept from his tent prior to sunrise half expecting to be alone; in fact, many of the guilds-men appeared never to have gone to bed. They sat huddled around the fire with cups of cider snuggled between both hands, visiting softly. Others, (those who had not been cleared as well as the women) led by Gregory, were already breaking down tents and loading down the mules. Ilandee, meanwhile, stood over Tiber's shoulder. Both were examining a small parchment in Tiber's hands, deep in obvious disagreement. Tagorin turned, expecting to see Dagon's tent, only to find it had already been packed away.

"We'll have to go through the pass," said Ilandee as Tagorin approached.

"The men won't like it," reasoned Tiber. "It'll be freezin' cold with the snow an' the wind."

"We have no choice," argued Ilandee. "The pass forks early on." He pointed to the map. "We can use that to our advantage. You will take your team to the left and mine will go right. Both routes exit near the relocation site, ten miles outside Finoval's boundaries."

"What of Gregory's team?"

"They are taking the Imperial Highway—nothing too suspicious: six mules, four horses (none ever belonging to the Empire), and one stagecoach. Larger parties have traveled the highway with no trouble."

"An' the Imperial horses?"

"I have a couple of men already at the next village trading the horses as we speak. They will rendezvous with Gregory's team as they pass through."

"All right, then," conceded Tiber. "The men'll still be upset."

"Precisely why you're breaking the news to them," announced Ilandee, clapping Tiber on the shoulder. Tiber opened his mouth and shut it again. He shook his head, muttered something foul, and walked over to Gregory.

"You're up earlier than expected," said Ilandee.

"I couldn't sleep," said Tagorin.

"I see. It's not all going to be fun and games, you know."

"I know."

"Good. Now, let's get some of this cider before it's all gone." Tagorin followed Ilandee to one of the barrels. Ilandee turned the tap and filled a cup for the both of them.

"Have you seen Dagon?"

"He's running an errand for Tiber," said Ilandee after taking his first sip of cider. He chuckled. "If Dagon isn't careful, he'll end up like Tiber—all work and no play."

"I heard you two talking about a pass."

"Oh yes, this will be your first time too." Ilandee smiled. "Well, we've never had reason to journey through the pass until now. Trouble is, we've become too familiar in this area—most villagers recognize us. It's getting difficult to trade in the area, and winter is approaching. Finoval is almost ideal to be near; access to the sea, more frequent trade, and more tolerable winters. There is also bigger risk—we'll have more direct confrontation with Felix and his Riders. We may have to split the company in half for the time being. Returning to your question, the pass isn't very long—a two-day journey—but as I'm sure you've gathered, very miserable. It climbs quickly and steeply, much of it is snow-covered, and a nasty wind frequents the summit."

"You've been there before?"

"Many, many times, I'm afraid, and each time more wretched than the first," said Ilandee after another long swig of cider. He gave the camp a quick gaze and motioned toward Tagorin's still-erect tent. "Best be getting ready."

Within the hour after sunrise, the camp was no more. The mules, now heavily loaded, dragged their burdens toward the Imperial Highway, followed by those who were not cleared to assist in the upcoming raid. Tagorin had quickly disassembled his tent and shoved it into his burlap sack along with his belongings: his pocketknife, his second shirt and pair of trousers, his newly acquired pair of deer-hide gloves, the remaining pint of honey mead, his seven silvers, one water-filled canteen, and the empty pouch that had contained the silver tree necklace that now hung around his neck. He had thrown on his worn traveling cloak and slung both his quiver and bow on his back.

At the head of the raiding party, Tagorin and Dagon trailed behind Ilandee and Tiber, who continued to exchange mildly heated discussion regarding procedures while most of the raiding party took no notice or care. Before long, the party had reached the shores of Lake Gray, and they took a momentary pause to fill their canteens at the calm headwater that fed the lake.

"I heard some of the men talking about the pass last night," said Dagon while they took their turns filling their canteen. "It's a two-day journey."

"Ilandee told me the same thing," Tagorin acknowledged.

"Some of them told me travelers have died on this pass before. Once, before the Imperial Highway existed, an entire royal trading party fell near the summit because they couldn't see — slipped right off the edge. No one ever found them."

"Ilandee did say the pass is miserable," conceded Tagorin, "but I doubt it's that bad. I mean, how does anyone know how an entire caravan disappeared if they never found them?"

"Dunno," said Dagon, fitting the cap on his canteen. "Just thought you should know — in case you want to change your mind about coming. I wouldn't blame you."

"Not a chance," said Tagorin.

Gradually, the company made its way through the Sigrún Forests and felt the first presence of chilled wind. A field of tall brown grass swayed in the wind before them, stretching for miles. In the distance, a series of large gray slabs shot up from the fog, reaching into the clouds. Tagorin wrapped his cloak tighter while Ilandee and Tiber gave one another a quick nod and pressed forward into the field and toward the Hackastine Pass.

CHAPTER FOUR: THE SECRET OF KING DEDALUS

Tagorin had never ventured out so far from the Sigrún. It came as quite a surprise when the Hackastine Mountains abruptly sprung from the land and into the clouds at midday. Massive and towering, the Hackastines loomed over the valley floor, casting everything into a shroud of darkness. Channeled wind bellowed from the deep canyons of the pass, carrying a cold so fierce that even Dagon (much to Tagorin's delight) had wrapped his cloak so thoroughly around himself that he had a difficult time walking.

The climbing had been quick—the flat field turned to rising hills and exposed cliffs to steeping switchbacks. Finally, there was a narrow path above a canyon, with room only for two side by side. Gusting winds ripped across the smooth canyon walls. The canyon itself was deep and bathed in shadow. Tagorin was accustomed to the dimness of Aldure's daylight hours, but even he was taken aback by the way in which the Hackastines absorbed what little light nature offered.

The Hackastines were barren. The wind alone would stifle the growth of even the most resilient plants. Animals did not flourish in the Hackastines as they had on the valley floor and in the Sigrún. The Hackastines were cruel—and yet here they were, men of flesh and sinew and bone, climbing ever higher toward the summit.

As the hours went by, the company was forced into a slow, single-file march up the narrowing corridor, the wind increasingly bitter and forceful with every step. The Hackastines quickly revealed the harshness of nature as smooth wind-carved slab sides turned jagged and coarse. Still, they marched one step at a time, higher and higher until they came to a large clearing within the canyon. The clearing was almost circular in shape, its vertical stone walls borrowed from the Hackastines. Here, some life had managed to grab hold. Trees hundreds of years old, their growth stunted by the harsh wind and bitter environment, stood no taller than Tagorin. Before them at the other end of the clearing were two openings. They had reached the fork.

"We'll rest here for the night," said Ilandee. "Pitch your tents on the perimeter of the clearing. The wind should be tolerable that way." No one spoke as tents were raised one by one while the wind whipped above them, roaring with an uncomfortable pitch. It was completely dark when all the tents had been erected. A small fire blazed at the center of the clearing, the wood harvested from what little the clearing provided. Everyone gathered at the fire, cloaks bound tight. It was the quietest night Tagorin had ever experienced.

"Reminds me o' the good ol' days," said Tiber unexpectedly, his voice calm and unhindered by the cold. He glanced at Ilandee, who nodded in agreement.

"The pass was never any better either," said Ilandee. "Might have been colder, but it's probably just wishful thinking."

"There'd be one difference," said Tiber. He paused a moment, eyeing the clearing walls, staring into crevice shadows. Ilandee nodded a second agreement.

"Wh-why?" Tagorin managed to ask. Both Tiber and Ilandee smiled a moment. Then, Tiber gave Ilandee an encouraging sideways nod as to voice a silent approval.

"Well," said Ilandee, "I'm sure you've heard of the demon knights before." Tagorin nodded.

"O-only heard of th-them," said Tagorin. "I never r-really believed it, though." Tagorin wrapped his cloak around him more tightly.

"Well, it's true," said Ilandee. "They are real." A wave of soft muttering traveled through the men. Tagorin caught a few of the words: *demons, wicked, foul, punished.*

"What are they?" asked Dagon, sitting on the other side of Tiber. "And how come I've never seen them?"

"You don' want to see 'em," said Tiber stoutly. "Trus' me on tha' one."

"Just tell me already," said Dagon. "I'm not scared." Both Tiber and Ilandee burst out laughing.

"Foolish boy," said Tiber.

"Tiber, don't excite him," said Ilandee. "Very well, I'll tell you." Ilandee reached for his canteen and took a long swig. He wiped his beard with his forearm and cleared his throat.

"You've heard, I'm sure, that when Dedalus claimed the Grand Throne, he did so to fill a void from the Grand King's death and to respond to the rebellion of many of the Jarls who once ruled in Aldure. You've heard this before, yes?" Tagorin and Dagon nodded. All the men had gone silent. It became quite obvious to Tagorin that many of the men had not heard this story either.

"It's all a lie," said Ilandee. The men erupted in quick whisperings. Again Tagorin heard bits and pieces.

"Told you so, didn't I?"

"But everyone knows about the rebellion. That wasn't no lie."

Ilandee waited for the men to quiet before he continued.

"Dedalus did not become king by circumstance—he was the rightful heir. His father was deathly ill, and before Alexander had even drawn his last breath, Dedalus staged a coup d'état. The rebellion that sparked over Aldure then was a response to this. However, Dedalus make quick sport of them, with their own blood."

"What does this have to do with demon knights?" asked Dagon.

"Patience," said Ilandee. "Have you never wondered how Dedalus was able to quell the might of nearly every kingdom in Aldure arrayed against him? You think he did this on his own? No, Dedalus played us all for fools, and when the time came, he took his place as the Grand King." Ilandee paused a moment and took another drink from his canteen.

"King Alexander had not intended Dedalus to succeed him on the throne. He had wanted Triton, his most outspoken critic among the Band of Kings, to watch over the throne until his daughter was old enough to rule. Triton, though very brash and critical, was loyal to the people of Aldure. And he was very loyal to Alexander, regardless of their numerous disagreements. As you can imagine, Dedalus did not want his claim challenged.

"Well, Triton did challenge him—not for the desire of the throne, but because he knew better than anyone Dedalus's cruel nature. Over half of the kingdoms in Aldure sided with Triton, and so the rebellion, as it is known, began. It was short-lived, however, as Triton and those who rose against Dedalus never stood a chance. Dedalus had a two-stage coup d'état ready. First, the secretive alliance between Knight Commander Felix Alric and Dedalus—no one saw it coming. White Riders in every city struck upon those who rebelled. At-tacked from within, they were unprepared for the attack that came from outside—the demon knights.

"You've never seen them, but they are real. They are not men, not anymore. It is believed only those with wickedness in their hearts can see them. They wear armor as black as night itself. Neither sword nor arrow can pierce their armor, nor the heaviest mace dent or scratch. They do not grow weary, they do not eat, they do not speak, and they do not sleep. They do not live, nor do they die. When they descended upon the rebellion, no man, woman, or child was left living. They know no mercy. The last to fall to Dedalus and his demon knights was the city of Ancleed. The rebellion hadn't lasted a day."

The fire had dwindled, and the men were qui-eter still.

"That's ridiculous," said Dagon abruptly. Ilan-dee gave him a curious smile. "That's just an old mother's tale to keep children home at dark."

"Hold your tongue, boy," said Tiber sternly. "You haven' heard the whole story yet."

"The reason you haven't seen them before,"

said Ilandee, "is because Dedalus keeps them in the mountains — these mountains, to be precise. The Hackastines run along the very spine of the land, from the southern fringes all the way north to the known world and probably beyond. We happen to be passing through the shortest pass of many that wind through these mountains. And as I said before: only those with wickedness in their hearts can see them." Ilandee paused a moment, turning so that he could stare directly at Dagon.

"They are his eyes, and his ears, and his fists. They move as shadows in the darkness of night. These are his weapons and the chains he clamps to the people of Aldure. For this reason, we travel through this pass as separate groups, in the hope that should one of us be discovered, the other will get through to the other side."

CHAPTER FIVE: THE OLD WAY

agorin slept miserably that night. Images of shapeless shadows wisped before his very eyes, all with swords and shields as the words echoed in Tagorin's mind: *They are his eyes, and his ears, and his fists.* Multiple times, Tagorin had found his hand resting on his bow, ready at a moment's notice to act. Eventually, out of exhaustion alone, he fell asleep, only to wake a few short hours later.

"Tagorin, get up," said Dagon. He flung the tent flap to the side and poked his head in. Tagorin groaned as he sat up and vigorously rubbed the tiredness from his eyes. Dagon paid no attention.

"Hurry it up. We have to move soon." Grumbling, Tagorin quickly dragged himself from his covering and crawled from his tent. It was still dark, but the camp was alive with movement as tents were torn down and garments and cloaks refastened and tightened. Like the night before, a pitiful fire sputtered at the center, where many of the men were gathered tightly around.

Tagorin quickly set about the business of his tent. He had asked Dagon for help but was brushed aside, the words *little boy* still ringing in his ears. Though shielded from most of the wind, the bitter air made the work of his tent a trying ordeal. The leather was stiff and uncooperative, and gloves made the task only more difficult. His fingers quickly turned a bright red as he rolled the leather (with great effort) back into the spool shape that fit on his pack. Nearly an hour had passed before Tagorin had fully deconstructed his tent. Much to his happiness, he found he was not the last to do so.

Light had just broken over the canyon, the darkness of the Hackastines washed away as much as any could have hoped, and the fire had sputtered its last flame of warmth. Ilandee and Tiber stood at the fork at the far end of the clearing, waiting for the men to gather.

"Tiber's group," announced Ilandee, his voice audible even with the whining wind above them. "You will take the left passage. Be careful, watch out for one another, and we will meet up in two days' time. There is an old, unused traveler's inn part way up the mountain on your path. You must reach that inn before nightfall, when the temperature drops. Once you reach the inn, the passage beyond is level, though very hazardous. Avalanches have claimed many lives in the area, so you must move slowly. You should be able to begin your descent on the second day, reaching an old scouting post before nightfall. From there, you will have a fast descent out of the pass and should reach the relocation site sometime around midday on the third day. Good luck."

Tiber's men quickly got into rank and file, and with little protest, followed Tiber down the left path. It took nearly an hour before Tiber's group had completely left the large clearing and disappeared from sight. Ilandee then turned to address his own men.

"We have our work cut out for us. Our path is shorter but more perilous. We will climb quickly. Unlike Tiber's group, we will reach the summit of this pass, and we must do so before nightfall. There is a temple at the peak of this pass that will shelter us from the harsh winds. We then have a sharp descent the second day — and this is where we must be very careful; one wrong step and it's over. With any luck, we will be out of these mountains before nightfall on the second day. We then have less than a half day's march to the relocation site." Ilandee turned to face them, pointing in the direction of the right passage. "I will warn you now — this path isn't just any passage; it's called the Path of Ten Thousand Stones." A dozen or more mutterings went through the group, but Ilandee paid them no attention.

"It's nothing more than what it sounds like; ten thousand stones made into steps, starting here, climbing to the summit, and then back down again. Be careful — the steps are slick, especially once we hit snow."

As they approached nature's daunting staircase, they passed a sign still intact at the base of the stony stairs:

Ahead you will climb
And after, descend
Toward the temple climb, climb, climb
Mind your step or you'll go
Down, down, down

Ascending the stone stairs was no easy task.

Uneven, brittle, and, in some cases, broken, the stairs were every bit as unrelenting as the Hackastines themselves had proved to be. They were narrow, so the company had to move in single file, which slowed the climb. Steps would collapse under foot, causing many to stumble. This slowed the climb further still, as everyone quickly became cautiously hesitant. With every step toward the summit, fog thickened around them, surrounding them in a blanket of gray. The wind persisted, growing more ferocious with every passing minute.

They moved forward, despite it all. They navigated the crumbling staircase step by step, often reaching out to the mountain walls to keep themselves from falling. Snow arrived more quickly than any of them would have liked, adding yet another element to their treacherous ascent. Snow buried the steps, making it even more perilous to reach the summit. The fog had been replaced by wind-blown snow, obscuring Tagorin's view of Ilandee in the process. Many times he had found himself reaching into the unknown and grasping the tail of Ilandee's cloak, just to be sure he was still there.

"I'm still here," shouted Ilandee, his voice barely audible over the gusting winds.

"Sorry," Tagorin shouted back, stumbling a little over a mixture of wet snow and debris. His feet were soaked from the snow, and his hands (though covered by gloves) were numb. Tagorin had never been so cold.

Tagorin lost all track of time as his feet rose and fell over and over again, his body growing in numbness with each step climbed. He could no longer feel his feet or his legs, though they carried him unmercifully up the mountain. As midday approached, all the feeling in Tagorin's body was gone.

Only once did Tagorin chance a quick look behind him. Tagorin noticed the man following him as a new recruit. The man's face was normally covered in a large red beard, in which dozens of small ice fixtures now lay embedded. The sight forced Tagorin to fix his gaze ahead of him once more. Hour upon hour, Tagorin marched up the stone stairs, all thought gone from his head. Light faded fast and the wind increased. He had even forgotten about the demon knights.

Just as Tagorin had lost all hope of ever being warm again, the ground leveled out. So lost was Tagorin in his numbness that he hardly noticed himself being guided toward a dark structure.

The stone temple stood solid against the raging wind. Its stones were cut from the Hackastines themselves, each block with its own harsh and unique shape. Tall but slender slits had then been carved out of the stone walls, allowing slivers of light to enter without compromise to the elements.

"Inside, quickly," shouted Ilandee, ushering everyone inside. The solid wooden doors were still intact.

"You too, come on," said Ilandee, grabbing Tagorin by the shoulder and rushing him inside. Tagorin stood in the hallway, or at least what he assumed to be the hallway. It was dark inside, and he could barely make out the shapes closest to him.

"Hurry, light the torches," said Ilandee. Tagorin could hear some of the men shuffling about their packs in search of turpentine. Soon after, light filled the temple. Tagorin found that he was not in a hallway but rather the atrium. He was further surprised that all fifty of them were able to fit comfortably inside.

Past the atrium, stone pillars were aligned in two evenly spaced rows extending the length of the sanctuary and standing nearly two stories high. It was a large temple for such a lonely place, spacious and easily accommodating to a hundred or more. Dozens of bookshelves lined the exterior walls of the sanctuary, most of them empty and many broken. At the opposite end of the sanctuary, the stone floor gave rise to a platform, upon which a podium stood still intact. Behind the podium hung a ripped banner, purple in color, though mostly faded. Tagorin felt his heart leap when he recognized the emblem on the banner; it was the broken tree, like the one on the necklace Ilandee had recently given him. He could not put into words the sudden connectedness he had gained with the temple. Indeed, he felt as if there were some secret here, a piece to a past he had never known.

But no one appeared to care about the temple or the hanging banner, as nearly every man had sat in the very place he stood and was tending to the coldness of his body. Ilandee was the only one present moving about the temple, smashing old bookshelves and tossing the broken scraps into the center of the sanctuary. He poured turpentine on the broken shelves and took his flint and set about starting a fire.

Moments later, a blazing fire roared to life, and with it, the chatter of the men who had abandoned their patch of cold wall in favor of the promising warmth. Tagorin too, lured by the crackling of the fire, left the banner on the wall and sat down next to the fire.

"These mountains were never any different," said Ilandee, taking a seat next to Tagorin. "Still, at least we all made it this far. Tiber and his men should be safe for the night as well." Tagorin held his hands to the fire, his numbness gradually fading.

"Why would anyone build a temple here?" asked Tagorin. Ilandee chuckled as he threw more wood onto the fire.

"They were built here to keep people away," said Ilandee. "This isn't any temple; it's a temple of the Old Way."

"The Old Way?" repeated Tagorin. "I don't understand."

"Well, I suppose you don't," said Ilandee. "And it's not exactly gone, is it? But all the same, we'll call it the Old Way. Rumor has it there are many temples like this one, built in hard-to-reach places, places where normal people wouldn't stumble upon them. You see, these temples guard something. I don't know what. Nobody does. Whatever it is, the builders didn't want normal people getting their hands on it. It's all legend of course, you understand."

"I guess," said Tagorin. "I don't see what is so special about this place."

"I don't know," said Ilandee. "I do know that the ones who watched over these temples fancied themselves as sages. They taught the Old Way to those who would listen. Their understanding of all things known and unknown fascinated men and women alike. It was not uncommon that the kings of old often held council with them."

"Where did they go?"

"No one knows," said Ilandee. "Some say our dear king is one of them. I don't know, but I wouldn't be surprised either. Hoethra's flags still bear the broken tree to this day, after all. All we know is the sages vanished without any warning sometime around the rebellion." Ilandee closed his eyes. Tagorin's heart sank—the unexpected connectedness he had felt with the temple vanished at the thought that he was somehow connected to Dedalus through his necklace. His hand moved unconsciously toward the necklace around his neck.

"So," said Tagorin, highly aware of the lump in his throat, "is that broken tree a symbol of the Old Way?"

"It is," said Ilandee. "But I wouldn't worry too much about that necklace of yours bearing the same image. Lots of stuff back then had that symbol. Lots of people believed in the Old Way, and some still do. "

"Do you," asked Tagorin, "you know, believe in the Old Way?" Tagorin, of course, didn't have the slightest idea what the Old Way was supposed to be.

"I don't know what I believe anymore," said Ilandee. "The world has changed so much in my time, I can't hardly remember what was good or bad back then, much less now. I think the Old Way was meant to be good, but somehow, we managed to turn it into something that isn't, something that it wasn't meant to be. Perhaps, the Old Way didn't change at all; it was we who changed. And when we couldn't recognize the Old Way anymore for what it was, we made our own way."

"Is that why the sages left?" asked Tagorin.

"Perhaps," said Ilandee. "Like I said before, no one really knows why they left."

"Ilandee?"

"Hmm?"

"Whatever happened to Alexander's daughter? You never said."

"No one knows," said Ilandee.

Tagorin woke the following morning stiff, with aches throughout his body. Despite his best efforts, he could do nothing to make the stone floor more comforting or inviting. His one small bit of comfort had been the blazing fire that had been tended throughout the night.

Breakfast was a silent one; no one spoke as each man rummaged into his pack for the little provisions he had brought for the short journey. Tagorin, however, had little time for breakfast, as his mind was thoroughly occupied by the remnant banner hanging in the sanctuary.

The fabric of the banner was frayed, worn, and faded, leaving little of the original purple dye intact. Multiple tears ran up and down the banner, further disfiguring the silver tree emblem. As on his necklace, there were unfamiliar letters arranged in a circular fashion about the tree. He desperately wanted to know the meaning of those letters.

"I can rip it down for you, if you like," said Ilandee, coming up behind him.

"Do you know what these letters mean?" asked Tagorin, pointing to one of the strange shapes. "They are the same ones on my necklace." Ilandee moved closer to the ancient letters and gave them a serious look-over. He stood there in silence for a few moments, only to shake his head.

"No," said Ilandee. "I'm afraid I'm not familiar with this language. Considering your necklace, this is only the second time I've seen this writing in my entire life."

"Is there anyone who might?"

"It's not impossible, but you shouldn't get your hopes up," said Ilandee, patting Tagorin on the shoulder. "We have a long day ahead of us; we'd best be going."

Tagorin was not eager to venture into the cold that waited outside the temple walls. Indeed, some of the crew motioned for another night's stay. Ilandee wouldn't have it. So, in the early hours of the morning, they left the temple (with significantly fewer bookshelves) and began their descent.

The descent was far more dangerous than the climb had been. No longer were they cradled between walls of stone. Now they treaded slowly along a narrow ridge on the mountainside. To their left was a smooth, wind-worn vertical mountain face, and to the right, certain death. They still faced the same uneven, brittle, and broken snow-covered steps as before, though this time with more caution and trepidation. One misstep, and it would all be over.

The wind beat savagely upon them, its iciness piercing their gloves and cloaks. They would halt with every unfamiliar sound and creak of the mountains: the frequent movement of loose debris and fallen rock, the quiet but definite thud of snow clumps falling from above, and sometimes the sudden absence of the wind.

But Ilandee had not led them astray — the descent was fast despite the pace at which they were forced to move. Every passing minute, they were aware of how much closer they were to the valley floor.

Eventually, Tagorin let his thoughts wander as the hours passed on. Images of the torn banner hanging in the temple flashed before him. He had the suspicion that Ilandee knew more than he had admitted, and he wondered why Ilandee would keep something so secret if he did indeed know. He wanted to know more about the Old Way and to know the secret words. Then his mind turned to Dedalus and the possibility he was a sage as Ilandee had mentioned. He wondered if the Old Way had been good at all. Soon his mind had run in circles and he no longer cared if the Old Way was good or not — the only thing that mattered was learning the secret words. *Then I will know*, thought Tagorin. *Then I will know whether it is good or bad.*

Tagorin had become so lost in his thoughts that he was surprised when Ilandee grabbed him around the waist and pushed him up against the rock face. The place he had been standing just seconds before had given way. The stone step beneath the loose snow and debris tumbled down the mountain with little impact. Tagorin took a moment to dare a glance down. He could see nothing. The whole valley was covered in mist. Ilandee took a deep breath and wiped his brow. After a minute or two, he motioned forward, and the men began again down the mountain ledge.

Startled from his near-death experience, Tagorin had resolved to keep his mind on the path ahead. He noticed too his own heightened response to the slightest lurches of the mountain, the subtle changes in the wind to the distinct steps of Ilandee behind him.

But their perseverance was rewarded. The snow had thinned and receded, and the wind had diminished considerably. The path widened and the switchbacks became more gradual and level. The mist had cleared, and they could see quite clearly in the distance the torchlights of Finoval. They had made it.

Just as the light was fading, they set up their tents at the very base of the mountain pass, careful to be well away from any wagon trails. The fire was lit, and the men (having regained their former selves from the mountain) gathered around and sang and drank and retold their stories of peril and danger. Exhausted from the long journey, Tagorin retired to his tent, forgoing the celebration. All he wanted was sleep.

The next day arrived quickly, and with it, a

rushed march to the meeting point. It was a short journey, just as Ilandee had said it would be. The ground was level and easy to walk, and the surrounding pines made a nice change of scenery from the harsh and bare Hackastines. When they had arrived at the meeting point, Tagorin was pleasantly surprised to find Gregory tending his cauldron and his crew already at work erecting the camp. A quick scan of the area told Tagorin that Tiber and Dagon's group had not yet arrived.

"They won't be too far behind," said Ilandee. He strode past Tagorin to speak with Gregory.

"Any trouble?" asked Ilandee.

"We was stopped by a scoutin' party, but they didn' give us any trouble," said Gregory, stirring his cauldron all the while.

"Any sign of Felix?"

"No," replied Gregory as he began cutting carrots into the boiling stew. Ilandee bent over the cauldron, nodding.

"Beef and carrots again?" asked Ilandee.

"There's corn too," snipped Gregory, his mustache quavering. "All with a dash o' salt."

"Just a dash?"

"An' no more," replied Gregory. "It'll be ready in a moment." Ilandee chuckled and took his seat near the cauldron fire, and they ate without word between them.

CHAPTER SIX: COMMANDER FELIX ALRIC

You should have seen him," said Dagon a few short hours later. "He screamed like a little girl; you would've thought he was dying." Ilandee chuckled as he ribbed Tiber with his elbow. Tiber had become quite cross.

"I didn'," said Tiber, his voice shallow but defiant. "You'd bellow an' holler if you were fallin' down a cliff."

"I suppose I would," said Ilandee. "But I'd have thought screaming would be far beneath you, Tiber." The three of them laughed yet again. Tiber's face swelled in anger.

"I tol' ya, I didn' scream," bellowed Tiber. Without uttering another word, he picked up his pace and marched ahead of them. Together, the three of them (led by Tiber at the far front) made their way along the Imperial Highway with caravans behind them. Nearly an hour passed before they reached the outer gates of Finoval.

The size of Finoval's walls left Tagorin speechless. The portcullis was wide and formidable, with two towers jutting up from each side, easily three or four stories in height. The gate itself was a crisscross of reinforced iron bars, with each intersection sporting a short but very sharp spike. In the towers, two White Riders stood, their bows drawn down upon them. At the gate itself, two mounted Riders took guard, a spear and shield to them each.

"State your business," said the guard to the left.

"Trade and the night's lodging," replied Ilandee.

"You're previous location?"

"South," said Ilandee. Tagorin rather thought Ilandee was fighting the urge to smile.

"City, please," said the guard shrewdly.

"Avlovan," replied Ilandee.

"What is your residency?"

"None," said Ilandee.

"None, you say," the guard replied, his eyebrows clearly raised.

"None," repeated Ilandee. The guard gave them another scowl then raised and cupped his hands to his mouth and shouted up toward the towers.

"Raise the gate." Each crank of the lifting mechanism screeched as the gate rose slowly off the ground.

"Gate open," shouted another voice from the towers.

"Come on, now," said Ilandee, grabbing Tagorin's shoulder and urging him forward.

"Last gate open at sundown," said the voice from the towers again.

Finoval was unlike anything Tagorin had ever seen. Wide cobblestone streets dispersed in all directions. People walked every which way, coming and going without rhyme or reason. Vendors of all sorts engaged in shouting matches, urging passersby to purchase the most recent goods. Buildings of various heights sprawled along each side of them, arranged in perfectly unified blocks. And that wasn't all: Pairs of White Riders appeared to be stationed at guard every other street.

"Do your best not to attract attention, and we'll

be fine," said Ilandee.

Tiber parted his own way through the crowd and was quickly out of sight. Ilandee then led the two of them through the maze of people and down a side street, while the main caravan set up shop amid the crowds. Away from the horde that had greeted them, Tagorin was able to fully absorb his surroundings. The streets were lined with lantern posts, which Tagorin had never seen before. They looked enough like lanterns, only they were slim and ornate, and the glass was etched with various images. There was no wick to light, nor was there a fount chamber for the oil.

"Marvelous contraptions," said Ilandee, pausing to look. "I haven't seen one of these in years."

"What is it?" asked Tagorin. Dagon too had stopped for a closer look.

"Well, obviously, it's a lamp," said Ilandee with a chuckle. "These go way back to the Old Kingdom. I never really understood how these worked, but they require no oil or wick. I believe they are called Azura lamps—bright as stars these are." Ilandee circled the lamp, his hand gently grazing over the glass.

"Come on," said Ilandee, gesturing onward. "You'll get a chance to see how it works at nightfall." They followed Ilandee down three different streets, each one narrower than the last. They had left the market district well behind and were in the depths of Finoval's residential area. The houses were much smaller than their market counterparts and seemed to have lost their unified and tidy structure. Many of the houses were made from brick that had aged well past its prime, paired with rotting timber.

Tagorin, however, did not have much time to ponder as Ilandee had stopped dead in front of them, his hands outstretched bracingly. Just yards away, a small crowd had gathered at one of the houses, its windows boarded and its door hanging crookedly. An elderly man, his torso exposed for lack of a shirt, sat on his steps with his face buried in his hands. A trio of White Riders towered over him. The first stood with a large purse in one hand, his other hand outstretched. He was clothed in a white robe with silver tassels around his neck—the identifying mark of an Imperator whose primary job was to collect taxes. The second, and more familiar of the three, stood with his hand resting on the hilt of his sword. Like the first, he also wore a white robe, but his was complemented by polished steel paladins, gauntlets, and a chest guard. The third, however, was very unlike the first two.

He stood at the center between the two, easily the tallest among them. A red cape flowed down the right-hand side of his uniform, concealing his right arm. His face was concealed beneath a hood that extended beyond his chest guard. Like the second, this one also had a sword though it was distinctly regal.

"Please, I have no more to give," said the old man, looking up at the Riders. The old man was clearly malnourished. But more noticeable were the multiple thin lacerations covering his back that appeared to have healed many times over. Tagorin suspected the wounds had been opened more than once.

"You are behind in His Majesty's Quality-of-

Life Assurance Tax," said the Imperator, his hand outstretched to such an extent it was nearly in the old man's face. "This tax promotes the equal and fair living conditions of all of Aldure's citizens as well as supports His Majesty's war effort to protect Aldure's citizens. Failure to pay this tax will result in exile from Finoval and the forfeiture of citizenship of Aldure. I urge you to pay the tax."

"Please," said the old man, "I am too old to work, and the food I have is begged."

"Furthermore," continued the Imperator, "a claim has been made against you for the secretive practice of the Old Way. You may be spared of the punishment by publicly renouncing this practice."

"Please," said the old man again.

"This will be your last opportunity to pay your dues of the tax and renounce this forbidden custom," said the Imperator.

"I cannot," said the old man, bowing his head in defeat.

"Then I hereby reclaim this property in the name of His Majesty, under the authority of the Imperium, and by the force of the Order of the White Rider." The first nodded to the second, who then grabbed the old man by the cuff of his wrists and pulled him to his feet.

"Please, have mercy," cried the old man, this time looking to the third, who had been silent and unmoved through the whole exchange. The old man wrestled free from the second Rider, falling to his knees before the third. The second Rider made to grab the old man, but the third lifted his hand to the guard. He then removed his hood and stared down at the old man.

His face was gaunt and pale, but no one would mistake the man as frail or weak. His hair was black with speckles of gray (as was the goatee) and was neatly trimmed. His chin was almost square-like, and his nose short and pointed. His eyes were dark, brown, and narrow. Tagorin thought for a moment the man might have been born from the Hackastines themselves.

"You know the law," said the third, crossing his arms. His voice was deep, and it carried authority and malevolence. "Why should you receive any special treatment that others are not afforded?"

"Please," said the old man. "I once was a Rider, a loyal servant of Alexander. Has it been so long that you have forgotten me, Commander?" It had now dawned on Tagorin who the man in the cape was: Commander Felix Alric. Tagorin had never seen him before, but he had heard enough stories around the camp to know well the commander's reputation and his many deeds.

"Heretic," bellowed the first Rider. "By decree of the Imperium and His Majesty's mandate, the name of His Majesty's predecessor shall not be uttered. Your words are the words of a traitor." Despite the Imperator's lecture, the old man did not cease.

"He chose you," said the old man, pointing accusingly at the commander. "He gave you the responsibility to defend justice and to protect the weak. You swore an oath—we all did that day." The commander did not move. He didn't so much as blink an eye.

"Is it not good to follow the law?" asked the commander. "Was not the law established for the good of Aldure? Is not the tax part of the law?"

"It is," answered the old man, standing on his own now. The second Rider had now drawn his sword in a threatening manner. The commander, however, remained as he had been.

"I would ask of you, is the law just?" Tagorin began to admire the old man. The old Rider's dormant spirit had reawakened. He may have been old, frail, and moments ago, on the verge of despair, but he spoke with new strength. Tagorin no longer doubted the man had once been a White Rider. In all his life, Tagorin had never imagined a Rider could be so...noble.

"Was it so long ago that you have forgotten how this land became great? Was it so long ago that men and women and those who served worked for the same purpose? Was is it so long ago that you and I swore an oath to protect those who could not defend themselves and to fight for what is right and just? I say *you* are the heretics! *You* are the traitors!"

The second Rider would have no more. He raised his sword in a second's time and brought it down hard. Tagorin braced for what he knew would come, what must happen. No sooner had he closed his eyes for the impact, he heard the distinctive clash of steel. He opened his eyes, surprised by the scene in front of him. The commander had drawn his own sword and parried the Rider's attack.

"C-commander," the Rider stuttered.

"Did I order you to run this man through with your blade?" asked the commander. The Rider did not move but stood paralyzed in a fashion Tagorin could describe only as fear.

"N-no, sir," said the Rider. "I-I only meant to defend His Majesty's honor, sir."

"And what exactly from this frail old man was threatening to His Majesty?"

"I—"

But before the Rider could reply, the commander heaved his sword with such force that the Rider was knocked to the ground. No sooner had the Rider hit the ground than the commander's sword was at his throat.

"You are henceforth stripped of your duty. You will turn in your uniform, and all the privileges associated are revoked."

"B-but, sir."

"I have killed men for questioning my orders," snarled the commander. At this, the commander sheathed his sword and returned his attention to the old man.

"We shall return this time tomorrow for the tax," said the commander. "I suggest you look extra diligently for any *misplaced* coin. You shall be publically lashed until you renounce your heretic ways."

"I think we've seen enough," whispered Ilandee. He gestured toward a nearby alleyway. They didn't get very far.

"Wait there, Ilandee," said the commander. Tagorin gave Dagon a nervous look. He took a small comfort to see that Dagon was also uncomfortable.

"I saw you coming down the street," said the commander, who was making a slow stride toward them. It was now that Tagorin was able to fully take in the commander's presence. He was very tall, easily Ilandee's height, possibly more. However, it was the sudden appearance of a slim smile that made Tagorin more worried than before.

"It's been a long time, yes?" asked the commander.

"Not long enough, Felix," replied Ilandee. He did not chuckle, nor did he smile. Rarely had Tagorin seen Ilandee so intense.

"You remember my name," said Felix, his smile broadening. "I'm very touched, particularly when I consider our last…disagreement." Felix than removed the steel-plated glove on his right hand, pointing to a burn on the backside of his hand.

Traitor

"I'm very sorry for that," said Ilandee. Tagorin was fairly certain he caught a glimpse of a smirk.

"I've no doubt," said Felix, replacing the glove over his hand. "I can't help but feel we didn't get to finish that quarrel."

"Oh, it's finished, I assure you," said Ilandee. "I'd say it's rather apparent the brand was appropriate." The commander smiled with a small nod. He then walked closely to Ilandee, leaned, and whispered in his ear. Tagorin, being near, didn't miss a word.

"I've heard it said a royal transport failed to arrive in Hoethra. I know it was you, Ilandee. But don't worry; I won't embarrass you in front of these children." He then leaned away and took one quick look at Tagorin and Dagon.

"Well, I suppose they aren't exactly children, are they?" He then looked and spoke directly to Tagorin, who throughout the ordeal had half hidden himself behind Ilandee. "Then again, this one isn't exactly a man, either." Felix smiled, patted Tagorin on the head, and laughed. The commander gave one last smile and nod to Ilandee and walked past them, followed promptly by the first Rider.

"Come on," said Ilandee, urging them forward and faster than before. "We'd best find a place to stay." Ten minutes, four narrow streets, and a dead end later, they had come to a tavern and inn. It was a couple of stories high, made of the same brick and timber as the surrounding houses. Tagorin was confident the building leaned to the right. On the front, a large sign read: The Leaning Tavern. Tagorin grinned.

"It isn't much," said Ilandee. "But it will do."

CHAPTER SEVEN: THE BARD

Night was nearly upon them as they stood outside the Leaning Tavern. The Azura lamps nearby had come to life, which was a pleasant surprise for Tagorin and Dagon. The light emanating from them was very bright, giving far more light than any lamp or torch Tagorin had used. Tagorin could easily have thought it was still daylight.

"I'll get us a couple of rooms," said Ilandee. "You two can wait outside if you like."

"I'll come," said Dagon. "You coming?"

"No," said Tagorin. "I'll wait outside for a bit."

"Don't wait too long," said Ilandee. "Felix is sure to be prowling around."

Tagorin nodded with his back to them, eyes glued on the Azura in front of him. Tagorin observed the Azura intensely, noticing the light was almost blue, much like the color of a very hot flame. Tagorin then set out to look more closely at the construction itself; he very much wanted to know how it worked.

He scanned the pole and the Azura itself completely, looking for knobs or dials or hidden lighting chambers, but he could find none. Frustrated, he turned his attention to the image etched in the glass. This one in particular had the image of a tree, very much like the one on his necklace. It was a repeated pattern, extending the entire circumference of the glass. Tagorin was then disrupted in his thoughts by a loud bang behind him.

The swinging doors of the Leaning Tavern had

crashed open. Three men stood in the doorway. A man far older than Tagorin had ever seen stood between two tall and rather hefty men, each holding the old man by his arms. The two men nodded to each other and threw the old man from the tavern. He flew ungracefully past the small flight of steps, landing heavily on the cobbled street. Behind the two men, framed in the doorway, stood the scariest woman Tagorin had ever seen, holding a wooden staff.

"I told ya, no more o' yer crazy stories, didn't I, ya crazy ol' man?" she bellowed, throwing the staff at the old man's feet. The old man lay like a crumpled heap at the foot of the tavern stairs, his hands raised and ready to defend himself as if the woman were advancing upon him with a weapon.

"I did not mean any harm," he said as his beard quivered with each word. "I tell stories only for fun and the enjoyment of others."

"No one likes yer stories," yelled the barmaid again. Her face became scrunched and her eyes disappeared beneath her thick eyebrows. She did not say it, but the look she gave the old man was clear: disgust. Tagorin, having seen enough misfortune for the day, walked up beside the man and lent him his hand. The old man looked up at Tagorin and took the outstretched hand. The old man was lighter than Tagorin had expected.

"Why ya helpin' that one?" the barmaid asked, shaking her head with great disgust. "He ain't worth th' trouble." She gave the pair of them one last reproachful look and wobbled back into the tavern.

"Thank you," said the old man, brushing the

dirt off his cloak. He was a peculiar-looking man, thought Tagorin. He wore white, loose-fitting garments (covered in stains and dirt). His cloak was brown and faded and ripped and patched in various places. Most striking was the thin scar across the old man's left cheek. Tagorin quickly found himself second-guessing Ilandee's decision.

"It is a nice place," said the old man with a broad smile. Tagorin raised his eyebrows at the old man. "Best food that can be found in Finoval, but its service is a tad on the rough side." The old man continued to smile, gazing intently at Tagorin.

"That is a very fine necklace you have there," said the old man, pointing to Tagorin's neck. Tagorin immediately grasped the necklace and stowed it back inside his shirt.

"Thank you," said Tagorin.

"My name is Pernic," he said, extending his aged and wrinkled hand. Tagorin met it with his own, surprised at how much strength the old man had in his grip.

"Mine's Tagorin."

"It is a pleasure, Tagorin," said Pernic. "Let me buy you a drink." He gestured toward the tavern he had just been thrown from.

"That's very nice of you, but um, weren't you just thrown out?" asked Tagorin. Pernic waved his hands dismissively.

"It is no matter," said Pernic, stooping down to retrieve his staff. "I will just promise not to tell any stories to those who do not like them." Reluctantly, and with the hope of escaping, Tagorin followed Pernic up the short flight of uneven stairs. Despite the building's worn and weathered appearance on the outside, its inside was warm and welcoming. A dozen or more square tables filled the middle of the room, lavished with decorated oil lamps and neatly folded napkins. A large, open fireplace crackled with flames at the far end. To the left, a bar counter ran the width of the tavern, behind which a flight of stairs climbed to the second landing. However, Tagorin's exploration of the tavern was interrupted yet again by the familiar bellowing of the barmaid.

"I thought I tol' ya, yer not welcome here," yelled the barmaid from the top of the stair landing. Heads turned to follow her staggered steps down the stairs. "I tol' ya I didn' want none o' yer nonsense in me tavern, didn' I?" Her nostrils flared wide, wrinkling the skin beneath her eyes. Tagorin rather thought she looked like a human pig.

"I simply wish to buy my friend a drink," said Pernic, raising his hands in a familiar fashion. "I give you my word not to tell any stories here. You will have no trouble from me." He fell silent and waited, his hands ready to defend himself a second time. The barmaid shook her head and turned her back to them, climbing the stairs from where she came.

"Come," said Pernic, gesturing to the stools next to the bar. Tagorin took his seat at the far end of the counter. Pernic leaned his staff against the counter edge between them.

"Two drinks," said Pernic to the bartender. He was a tall, stout man with a long and bushy gray mustache. "Honey mead would be preferable." The bartender ducked down behind the counter, slid open a door, and made a few banging noises Tagorin thought were quite unnecessary. When the bartender resurfaced, he held two small glasses in his left hand and a heavily dusted bottle in his right. He set the glasses down uncaringly and poured the soft golden liquid without grace.

"Thank you," said Pernic, placing two silver pieces onto the counter. The bartender snatched them up and dropped them into his pocket. Pernic then raised his glass to Tagorin. "To your health." Tagorin gave a quick nod and quickly took a sip of his mead.

"Tell me, Tagorin," said Pernic, "I have never seen you around before. From where do you visit?" Tagorin coughed slightly on his mead. Tagorin's heart skipped a beat as he tried to remember what Ilandee had told the guard at the gates.

"South," replied Tagorin. He took another sip from his mead.

"'It is a secret, then," said Pernic with a quick smile. Tagorin took a third, longer drink from his mead.

"You should not drink so fast, my friend," said Pernic with a chuckle. "Men greater and wiser than you or I have met their end in a bottle." Tagorin did not respond but resisted taking another drink. Tagorin was beginning to worry — Pernic was becoming too nosy. Tagorin needed to get away quickly.

"You know," said Pernic, "I have not seen a necklace like yours in a long time."

"You've seen one before?" asked Tagorin, forgetting his reservations toward the old man.

"Oh yes," said Pernic, reaching down into his shirt. A moment later, Pernic was holding an almost identical necklace in his hand. Tagorin could not believe his eyes.

"Does it have, you know, strange letters around it?"

"Strange letters?" repeated Pernic. "Nonsense." He showed his necklace to Tagorin. The letters were identical to those found on his own necklace.

"These are the same as mine," said Tagorin. "Look." Tagorin showed his to Pernic.

"Of course they are," said Pernic, taking another sip of his mead. "They would not be the same otherwise."

"But they both have strange letters."

"Perhaps it is you who are strange," said Pernic. "The words could not be clearer."

"What do they say?" Tagorin could feel his heart racing. Ever since he had been given the necklace, knowing the words had occupied his thoughts more than anything ever had. Tagorin could not believe his luck; this complete stranger was about to reveal all to him.

"I'm not telling," said Pernic. "It is a secret." Tagorin felt his heart drop.

"Why?" asked Tagorin.

"Because it is," said Pernic. "Besides, it has long been the tradition of old people to make young people squirm in discomfort when they do not know an answer."

"That's the stupidest thing I've ever heard," said Tagorin. "What kind of rule is that?"

"A secret one," repeated Pernic, smiling this time. "At least it was for a time—not so much anymore, is it?" Tagorin was rather disappointed. He had been so close to learning the secret words. And then Tagorin remembered the reason Pernic had been thrown from the tavern.

"You like to tell stories, right?"

"Oh yes," said Pernic, raising his glass at the bartender. There was a pause while the bartender waited on Pernic, filling his glass with a second round of honey mead.

"What kind of stories?" asked Tagorin when Pernic did not elaborate.

"Oh, a little of this, a little of that, and quite a bit of that over there," said Pernic, gesturing outward.

"There's always been a story I've wanted to hear, but no one has ever been able to tell it to me," said Tagorin. Pernic took another sip of his mead.

"Oh?" And what story is it that fascinates such a young mind as yours?" asked Pernic.

"The Old Way."

Pernic, who was in the midst of raising his glass for yet another drink, paused and — in what appeared to be a very forced action — set his glass gently on the counter. The bartender looked up suddenly, his eyes wide. Pernic gave him a small smile then returned his gaze to Tagorin.

"The Old Way, you say," said Pernic, his voice now a whisper. "It is a story I know well, and a story I take great care in keeping...discreet. You see, though it is a marvelous story, it is not well received. And you should take extra caution not to mention it at all — at least not in taverns where it is easy to be overheard."

"Is that why you were kicked out earlier?"

"Perhaps, perhaps not," said Pernic. "At any rate, it is a story I am not willing to tell." Frustrated, Tagorin turned away from Pernic and continued instead to examine his necklace. He had been so close.

"I am curious, though," said Pernic, his voice still low, "how you even came to know of the Old Way. The Old Way is from a time before yours, long forgotten by those who once believed."

"Someone told me the necklace was related to it," said Tagorin, careful not to reveal sensitive information. Ilandee would be quite cross if he started spouting carelessly. "That's all I know."

"Tell me, Tagorin," said Pernic, "how did you come into possession of this necklace?"

"It was given to me," said Tagorin, choosing his words carefully. He still wasn't sure if Pernic could be trusted. "I was told it had belonged to my parents."

"You're an orphan?"

"Well," said Tagorin, "my parents aren't around, if that's what you mean. I have a family."

"I see," said Pernic, his voice trailing off. He took another sip of his mead before continuing.

"Right," said Pernic. "I have decided to break tradition, seeing as I have made you properly frustrated."

"You'll tell me the words?"

"Heavens no," said Pernic. "That would not do at all, would it? It would take all the fun from the mystery, yes? No, I shall tell you instead a different story — not the one you wanted to hear, but a story related nonetheless."

Tagorin was left feeling rather disappointed.

"Come now, chin up," said Pernic, who was smiling quite jubilantly now, causing the scar on his cheek to become very disfigured. The look was nearly unsettling to Tagorin. "I promise you shall not be disappointed."

"Fine," said Tagorin. He would listen to the old man's story, and then, as soon as he could, he would excuse himself to find Ilandee.

"That is the spirit," said Pernic, raising his glass to Tagorin. "Now, the story I am about to tell you is an old one, and a very important one. It is nearly as dangerous of a story as the Old Way. Tell me, Tagorin, have you ever heard the story of how humans came to Aldure?"

"No," said Tagorin. "Haven't we always been here?"

"Not at all," said Pernic. "Once, this land had no name at all—or at least, no human name. This was all well before your time, or mine for that matter, you understand? Time was still young then. We came from another land—a harsh land—a land starved of fertile ground and clean water. And we were slaves, Tagorin, slaves living under the hand of a tyrant. You must understand that hope is what keeps us going.

"It was told to our ancestors that a time would come when they would inherit a land of great resources, a land with bountiful water and fertile ground, and, more importantly, they would be free. And so one day, one of our ancestors, a banished man, returned and led our people free. They journeyed through many strange lands over the course of many years."

"Are you saying that Aldure is the land in this story?" asked Tagorin.

"Oh, most assuredly it is," said Pernic. "Aldure

is where our ancestors settled. It is how we came to be here."

"You said this story is dangerous," said Tagorin, remembering Pernic's earlier statement.

"It is," said Pernic. "You see, it was our ancestors who brought us the Old Way." Tagorin could no longer contain his excitement.

"Tell me," said Tagorin. "Please."

"Well—" began Pernic, but he was interrupted by a sudden scream from outside the tavern. The tavern feel silent as heads turned toward the swinging doors. The woman barmaid thundered down the stairs, halting at the bottom step. A few moments passed, and some of the patrons of the tavern resumed their conversations. Then came a second scream, closer and higher pitched than the first. The tavern fell silent once more. Pernic took hold of his staff, his eyes fixed on the swinging doors. Then, many things happened all at once. A series of screams erupted, and the swinging doors of the tavern slammed open. A slender figure stood framed in the doorway, a sword sheathed at the side. Pernic stood as the person (clearly a woman) removed the hood covering her face.

Tagorin gazed at the young woman. Her hair was long and almost perfectly straight, its color very nearly as blond as his own. Her eyes, Tagorin noticed, were oddly bright, much like the blue of the Azuras outside.

"White Riders," said the woman softly and directly to Pernic. "They are attacking the city."

CHAPTER EIGHT: RIDERS ATTACK

No one moved or said a word; they all stared at the mysterious woman. Then it came again— the sad, echoing ring of the shipyard bell, followed by ear-piercing shrieks that spread through all of Finoval. Chairs were strewn across the floor as patrons jumped from their seats, pushing and shoving their way toward the swinging doors. The barmaid was the most ferocious, screaming in her horribly deep voice as she easily flung men to the ground on each side of her. The bartender followed closely behind, easily making his escape with the widened path of the barmaid.

"Where are they now, Enora?" asked Pernic over the noise of the tavern.

"All over," said the young woman briskly. Tagorin had yet to take his eyes from her. Enora was dressed to do battle. Her tight-fitting leather garments were heavily layered with straps that held various knives and an assortment of other things Tagorin had never seen before. Despite this, Tagorin rather thought the young woman was stunning. Had Tagorin not seen her as she was now, he would never have imagined her burdened by so many blades.

"We must not linger then," replied Pernic, taking the last sip from his glass. Just then, from the opposite side of the room, Ilandee and Dagon had emerged with a dozen other tenants of the inn.

"Ilandee," said Tagorin, running over to meet them. Ilandee placed his hand on Tagorin's shoulder but talked instead to Pernic.

"It's been a long time, Pernic," said Ilandee, nodding.

"It has," said Pernic, returning an equal nod. "I am sure introductions are in order, but we have more pressing matters to deal with. Who is the informant?"

"One of mine, I'm afraid," said Ilandee. "What's the plan?"

"We must make it to the ship quickly if we have any chance of escape," said Pernic. "It would be best to go different routes and meet at the ship."

"I'll take this one," said Ilandee, nodding to Dagon. "I'll leave Tagorin to you. And of course, you'll be needing this." He handed Pernic a sealed parcel.

"But—"

"Trust him, Tagorin," said Ilandee. "He's an old friend. You're in good hands. I will meet you at the ship."

"It has come to pass, Ilandee," said Pernic. His eyes suddenly narrow. "It is no longer safe." Without another word, Ilandee guided Dagon swiftly from the tavern. Dagon glanced back to Tagorin and was gone.

"You are familiar with the White Rider Order, I presume," said Pernic, readjusting his cloak. Tagorin nodded.

"Then I feel you will agree it best for us to go," said Pernic, motioning forward with his staff.

"But what about Ilandee and Dagon?" asked Tagorin.

"We will see them soon, all things considered."

"We don't have time for this," snapped Enora. She glared at Tagorin.

"This young man did me a kind service earlier, and it is only proper to assist him. At any rate, it was the request of an old friend."

"*Fine*," said Enora. She turned her gaze again toward him. "If you don't move now, I'm going to cut open your spleen and leave you as a welcoming gift to His Majesty, understand?" Tagorin became keenly aware of his own space and the distance between himself and Enora. He quickly agreed to go with them.

"Excellent," said Pernic, who despite the seriousness of the moment wore a look of amusement.

"Let's go," said Enora, leading the way from the tavern.

Finoval was in complete disarray. People ran frantically in all directions. Traders were more hysterical; some had given up on their donkeys or mules and pulled their own carts along the streets. Some abandoned their carts altogether, taking with them only coins.

"This way," said Pernic, pointing to a side street. The light from the nearby Azuras was enough to navigate through the darkened streets. But that did not remain the case for long.

"It would be best to move in the dark," said Pernic, nodding to Enora. She returned the nod and ran in front of them, her blade now held firmly in both hands. One by one, she brought the broadside of her sword into the Azuras, placing their route in complete darkness.

"We will need an alternative route to the docks," said Pernic. "The main will be sealed off already."

"I know of another," replied Enora, jumping

over a fallen cart. Tagorin attempted to follow suit but was caught by the wheel and fell face-first. Enora glanced over her shoulder but didn't stop. Pernic did not bother with jumping the cart; rather, he simply slowed to a fast walk and stepped over one of the handles and lent Tagorin an outstretched hand.

"You will have to forgive her," said Pernic. "She is not normally so shrewd. But come, or she will leave us both to fend for ourselves." Tagorin nodded and followed Pernic into the second stretch of the narrow street. Three times Tagorin was nearly knocked to the ground by passing crowds, saved only because Pernic continuously grabbed the scruff of his shirt. They turned left down a wider street and right again down another narrow strip. Tagorin had yet to see Ilandee or Dagon.

Another scream came from their left. Pernic darted his head, and Tagorin looked as well. Three White Riders charged down an intersecting street with blood-drenched spears clasped tightly in their hands.

"Hurry," shouted Enora, as she ducked into yet another narrow street of tightly compacted buildings. They were now in the market district. They weaved their way through two more stretches of road, somehow avoiding the White Riders galloping past. The docks were close now.

"There is a narrow path used by the guard of the city," said Enora. "It's a tunnel that travels along the seaside wall. It will probably be locked, but I should be able to get us in." They made three more turns through the market district side streets. Finally, they reached the seaside wall and the iron bar gate leading to the tunnel. Enora tried the latch; it was locked.

"This will take some time," said Enora, pulling out a small pouch and unrolling it on the ground. A dozen or so different lock-picking tools were stored inside. Enora immediately set to work on the gate.

"You don't have much time," said Pernic. His gaze darted from street to street. A massive formation of White Riders and their steeds raced down the wide center street of the market district, launching their spears airborne into the gathered crowd and drawing swords from their scabbards.

"I can work only so fast," snapped Enora.

"Is this the only route to the ship?" asked Tagorin, thinking of Ilandee and Dagon.

"Other than the main one, yes," said Enora.

"Your friends will be fine, Tagorin," said Pernic. "Ilandee is quite capable."

"How do you know Ilandee?" asked Tagorin. "I've known him my whole life, and he never mentioned you once."

"A story for another time," said Pernic. "Let's make it to the ship first."

"Blast," shouted Enora. One of her tools had snapped clean in two.

"Enora, we are short of time," said Pernic.

"Perhaps you would like to do it?"

"No, that is quite all right," said Pernic. "I wish only to stress the limited time we have." Enora ignored him and continued her work on the lock. Then, something caught Tagorin's attention from the corner of his eye. Down the next street, Ilandee was running full bore. Then, quite distinctly, he heard Ilandee yell, "Dagon."

Tagorin bolted for the nearby street.

"Tagorin, wait," shouted Pernic, but Tagorin ignored him.

"Ilandee," shouted Tagorin, his eyes fixed on Ilandee's back. He ran down the narrow alleyway, no longer paying heed to the nearby Riders or the screams of the city or the blood that now stained most of the streets.

"Ilandee," shouted Tagorin for a second time. Tagorin could hear Pernic close behind as well. Ilandee, however, showed no signs of slowing. The gap between them grew steadily with each passing intersection.

"Ilandee," shouted Tagorin for a third time. No answer came, but still he forced himself onward. Ilandee was now hardly visible in the darkness of the city. He did not know what Ilandee was chasing, and he had seen no sign of Dagon either. And then Ilandee had stopped. Tagorin quickly lunged forward, desperate to reach Ilandee. And then he saw them: five White Riders, one of them recognizably Commander Felix Alric, and another distinguished man garnished in a red robe. Between two of the Riders was Dagon, his wrists tightly bound. Tagorin, not more than an intersection away, readied himself to leap to Ilandee's side. Just as he prepared to do so, Pernic caught him around the waist and covered his mouth with a hand.

"Quiet," said Pernic. He then released Tagorin and turned his gaze toward Ilandee.

"Let him go," said Ilandee.

"So good to see you so soon, Ilandee," said Commander Alric. "I was rather hoping we'd have a chance to talk about the old days."

"Let him go," said Ilandee again. "He's just a boy."

"This one?" said Alric, ruffling Dagon's hair. "I think not."

"Let him go," said Ilandee, only this time in a voice Tagorin had never heard before. It was harsh — threatening.

"You mean to save him, do you?"

"I will," said Ilandee. The Riders laughed this time. This time, the man in the red robe spoke. His voice was raspy and short of breath. He was bald and from what Tagorin could make out in the dark, had a very pointed nose.

"Do you remember me, Ilandee?" asked the man in red.

"Let him go," said Ilandee. Tagorin watched as Ilandee drew his knife. This drew further laughter from the Riders.

"Straight to the point as ever," said the man in red. "I remember you well, Ilandee. Tell me, are you still mad about the death of your brother?"

"He is about to be avenged," said Ilandee. "I will make you pay for your crimes, Ortho."

"He begged, you know. Pleaded for mercy."

"You're a liar," shouted Ilandee. He made a step forward as one of the Riders also stepped from the ranks. He removed his hood — it was Tiber.

"Now don' do anythin' rash, Ilandee," said Tiber. Tagorin made to move, but Pernic grabbed him yet again.

"How much, Tiber?" asked Ilandee. "How much did they pay you?"

"It was never 'bout the money," said Tiber.

"I'll take care of you as soon as I've finished with the rest," said Ilandee, his voice shaking now. "I'll save you for last."

"Fool," said Ortho. "You think you can kill me? Your brother thought the very same."

"I'm not afraid of you," shouted Ilandee, lunging full force at the man in red; there was a blinding red light accompanied by the sound of echoing thunder, a yell, and a soft thud.

CHAPTER NINE: A NEW TIDE

Nothing happened; Tagorin was sure of that. It was some trick the men had planned all along to get away; that was why he couldn't see. The red glare subsided and the cold darkness of the streets came back into focus. Ilandee lay facedown on the cobblestone.

"Ilandee," shouted Tagorin, breaking free from Pernic's lax grip. He ran to Ilandee and fell to his knees beside him. He had fallen, Tagorin reassured himself. He was going to roll over on his back any moment now and laugh as he always did. And then those men were going to be sorry.

But Ilandee didn't move.

He must be unconscious, thought Tagorin. That was it; he had fallen over, taken by surprise of the blinding red light, and hit his head on the cobblestone.

"Ilandee," said Tagorin forcibly. He shook Ilandee as hard as he could, but still Ilandee did not stir.

"It's no use, child," said Ortho, bending down on the opposite side of Ilandee, gazing directly into Tagorin's eyes. Only now had Tagorin glimpsed Ortho's face in its entirety. His face and forehead were lined with scars, many deep and improperly healed. It was his blazing red eyes, however, that Tagorin found frightening.

"What did you do?" demanded Tagorin as he shook Ilandee again. "Why won't he wake?"

"Oh, dear," said Ortho, reaching a hand out to Tagorin's shoulder. Tagorin pushed it away. "It is a terrible thing I'm told — to lose someone close. That is why it's best not to care for anyone."

"Wake him up," demanded Tagorin. "Wake him up." Ortho then reached out with both hands and forced Tagorin to look him in the face.

"He's dead, child," said Ortho, his head crooked to one side now. "You don't want the same to happen to you, do you?" Ortho then took his right hand and placed it on Tagorin's forehead.

"Don't be afraid, child," said Ortho, a smile forming on his face. "Soon it will all be over."

"That is far enough, Ortho," said Pernic, stepping out from the shadows. Ortho hastily stood again, his blazing red eyes dancing at Pernic's sudden appearance.

"Don't be a fool, old man," said Ortho. "You're outnumbered and embarrassingly, outclassed."

"This old fool still has a trick or two," said Pernic as he moved between Tagorin and Ortho.

"You know whom I work for," said Ortho. "You can't hope to win. You had your chance, Pernic. You failed. It's a new era — your race has been run."

"It is far from over, Ortho," replied Pernic. "I have a message for His Majesty: It has begun. Step down while you still have that opportunity." The Riders laughed, but Ortho silenced them with a quick glare.

"I suggest you not follow us," said Ortho. He gave another quick look at Tagorin, his expression similar to hunger. "We will meet again, child." They turned and started down the next street. Then Tagorin remembered Dagon.

"Wait!" shouted Tagorin as he made to follow

them. "Dagon!" But Pernic swiftly restrained him.

"Let me go!"

"I cannot allow it, Tagorin," said Pernic.

"I said let me go!"

"No."

"They have Dagon!" shouted Tagorin. He continued to struggle in Pernic's arms until he felt something heavy hit him over the head. Then—nothing.

"It worked, didn't it?"

"There are better ways to gain trust."

"Then maybe he'll remember that the next time he wanders off like he did."

"That is not the point, Enora." Tagorin stirred at the name. His vision was fuzzy and blurred, but wherever he was, he was warm and cozy. He was on a bed, covered in blankets. He could smell the salty sea air around him. He thought of moving, but his body did not follow. More voices floated from beneath him.

"Should we wake him?"

"No—let him rest while he can." Tagorin's eyes were heavy, and he could fight them no longer. His eyes closed and he drifted again.

Tagorin woke the second time to a barrage of noise above and beneath him. His eyes flung open. Above him was a wooden ceiling. He made to rise, but a hand on his chest had guided him gently back to the bed. It was Pernic.

"Glad to see you awake, Tagorin." The old man smiled down at him. Pernic stood at the side of his bed, leaning on his wooden staff.

"Where am I?"

"On a ship, heading to the city of Zythan," said Pernic. "It will be a short stop on our way to Ancleed." And then Tagorin remembered.

"Where's Ilandee?" he asked, bolting up so suddenly that Pernic was unable to react.

"He's here," said Pernic, doing his best to urge Tagorin back onto the bed.

"He's all right?" asked Tagorin, calming a bit. Pernic didn't respond immediately.

"I'm sorry, Tagorin," Pernic finally said. "Ilandee has left this world." Tagorin fell silent. It had all happened so fast.

"What will happen to me?" asked Tagorin. "And what about Dagon?"

"We can discuss that once you have some food in your stomach."

"I want to see Ilandee," said Tagorin, shaking his head at the thought of food.

"Very well," said Pernic. "Follow me." Pernic led him from the room, taking a left down a narrow hallway. They descended a small flight of stairs. Tagorin was sure they would soon be in the cargo hold of the ship. Pernic then guided him through another door and into a pitch-black room. A few moments passed as Pernic shuffled about. Tagorin heard the tinkering of glass and the lighting of a match. Soon a dim light flickered from the candle lamp, which Pernic held at arm's length in front him. Slowly Pernic led Tagorin along the room, passing various crates and barrels. Then, in the corner of the cargo hold, Tagorin saw the outline of body lying atop a row of crates, covered in white linen. Tagorin walked up beside the body, his hands hovering slightly above the sheets. He paused a moment, unsure of what to do. Then, with great effort, he slid the sheets down to reveal Ilandee's face.

Gingerly, Tagorin traced the outline of Ilandee's face. Utter surprise was etched in every line of his face; Tagorin knew because he had seen it so many times before, such as when he had shown Ilandee the first-ever bow he had made, as well as the time when he had emerged from the river alive when he couldn't swim. It was the same surprised look Ilandee had given when he and Dagon emerged from the forest, victorious over the White Riders.

Along with the surprised expression was a slim smile, frozen in time with rest of his existence. Ilandee had not been afraid; Tagorin was confident about that. He even suspected that Ilandee had fully expected to walk away with Dagon securely by his side. But it had not happened that way. Ilandee was dead and Dagon was gone.

He had never asked Ilandee about matters concerning death. Never had the thought crossed his mind, though he had been close to death many times before. Now he felt as though the answer had left him along with Ilandee. He curled his fists and slammed them into the edge of the crates that held Ilandee. Over and over, he beat his fists into the crates as the truth flowed over him in one over-powering sweep. Tagorin fell to his knees, his hands red and throbbing from his frivolous battle with the crates. All at once a dozen questions flooded his thoughts, all of them without answers and each question giving rise to another. He felt alone.

So lost was Tagorin in his grief that he barely noticed Pernic guiding him from the cargo room and back up the flight of stairs. They walked a second time down the narrow hallway (passing the room Tagorin had slept in) and climbed another set of stairs. Pernic had led him into the ship's cabin.

The cabin was considerably spacious, though dimly lit with oil lamps. A few port windows let slivers of light in as well. Pernic led Tagorin over to a table at the far end of the cabin where Enora was already sitting. Tagorin nodded to her, but she simply continued to stare out the window. She was the only person around.

"Here," said Pernic, placing a pewter plate in front of him. On it was a modest-size slice of bread, a small hunk of cheese, and a clump of grapes. Pernic then also placed a small goblet of water on the table before sitting himself next to Tagorin. Tagorin eyed the food in front of him. He was aware that his body was hungry, but the thought of food only made him sick.

"Tagorin, you must eat," said Pernic.

"How long have I been out?" asked Tagorin.

"Half a day," said Pernic. "We've been at sea for nearly six hours."

"I don't remember boarding," said Tagorin, his finger tracing the lip of his goblet.

"Ah," said Pernic with a quick smirk. "That is because you were unconscious. Compliments of Miss Enora here." Tagorin took another glance toward her, but still she stared out the window.

"You see," continued Pernic, "you were nearly uncontainable by my efforts alone, so Enora — rather wrongly, I must say — clubbed you over the head with a broken wagon handle." Slowly, the previous night's events came into focus in Tagorin's mind. He remembered a red light, a man named Ortho, and Ilandee.

"Who are you?" asked Tagorin, his voice louder than he expected. "And why did you save only me? And what about my friend, Dagon?"

"Please keep your voice down, Tagorin," said Pernic. He gave a quick scan of the room before continuing. "I understand how upset you must be, but saving you was my only priority. It was Ilandee's priority also."

"How do you know Ilandee?" asked Tagorin, remembering the brief conversation in the Leaning Tavern.

"It is a marvelous tale," said Pernic, shifting in his seat and stretching his back. He leaned toward the table, his hands resting on the head of his staff. "But before I begin my story, I must ask you a question, Tagorin. Do you wish to save your friend?"

"Of course," said Tagorin. For a brief moment, he envisioned himself storming a fortress wall, singlehandedly destroying those who had been responsible for Ilandee's death and Dagon's capture. Then, almost immediately afterward, his thoughts turned to Ortho and his blazing red eyes and how easily he had dispensed with Ilandee. Defeat sunk into his heart.

"You hesitate," said Pernic.

"I don't know what to do," said Tagorin. "I can't fight people like Ortho."

"My dear boy," said Pernic, shaking his head, "it is not just Ortho you must face to save your friend; you must face the king himself." Tagorin felt his heart sink and his throat tighten. His breathing had become quick and short, and his heart knocked at his chest. Then, Pernic placed his hand on Tagorin's shoulder.

"Facing the king is no small feat," said Pernic. "You will not be alone."

CHAPTER TEN: REBELLION REBORN

I met Ilandee long ago," said Pernic as he twisted one of his long fingers in his beard. "It must have been nearly thirty years ago—met him in the city of Zythan, which is where we are heading now. He was the middle child of three, all brothers. You might find it hard to imagine, but he was of royal blood. Ilandee's father was a distant cousin of King Alexander, whom Ilandee later served as an ambassador."

"I know that name," said Tagorin. "He was the Grand King."

"Yes," said Pernic with a nod.

"And Ilandee said Dedalus was Alexander's son."

"Indeed," said Pernic. "Tell me, Tagorin, what do you know about King Dedalus?"

"Well," said Tagorin, thinking a moment, "he is cruel, and Ilandee said he took the throne by force, even though he was the rightful heir. But there is one thing that Ilandee told me that I don't quite understand."

"What is that?"

"Ilandee told us that he controls a huge army of demon knights."

"So you *have* heard of them."

"They're real?"

"Oh yes," said Pernic. "As real as you can imagine, Tagorin."

"Why haven't I ever seen one, then?"

"It is a simple matter of awareness," said Pernic. "They are everywhere. They were in Finoval, to be sure."

"I don't understand," said Tagorin. "I never saw any of them."

"Consider yourself fortunate," said Pernic. "At any rate, it is enough for the moment that they are real. Saving your friend is a more immediate concern."

"What does Dedalus want with Dagon?"

"For any number of reasons, I imagine," said Pernic. "But you can be assured there is purpose to the deed. Dedalus is not one to act without a plan. Saving your friend will require much, Tagorin. It may even require your life."

"I understand," said Tagorin.

"Very well," said Pernic. "It is important, I think, that you know a bit more about our king. You are aware, or at least have heard, of the Old Kingdom?"

"Yes," said Tagorin. "I've heard lots of stories about the Old Kingdom. The Grand King ruled Aldure with the Jarls."

"Yes," said Pernic. "They governed from the Magistrate in the capital city of Hoethra, where the Grand Throne resides and the birthing place of the White Rider Order. Aldure still resembles much of the Old Kingdom. For instance, all the major cities—called the Twelve—are still present and inhabited. However, Aldure is no longer united, nor is it the peaceful land it once was.

"As you are no doubt aware, Dedalus has firm control over the westward provinces and the cities that reside there. Eastward, Jarl Triton has so far held Dedalus at bay, but his army and resources grow weary. It is only a matter of time before

Dedalus prevails."

"I thought Triton died in the rebellion," said Tagorin. Ilandee had told him the rebellion hadn't lasted a day.

"Not at all," said Pernic. "Triton is a shrewd and careful man. He will not go down easily. As I was saying, Aldure is no longer united, and a second rebellion is preparing to strike. If there is any hope to save your friend, you will need the opposition."

"Is that what you are doing?"

"Enora and I are already part of the rebellion," said Pernic, nodding to Enora. "We were in Finoval to meet with Ilandee, who had gathered vital information on the common supply routes used by Dedalus and his White Riders."

"You mean—"

"Yes," said Pernic. "Ilandee has been a part of the rebellion since the beginning."

"But now he's gone," said Tagorin. "And so is the information you need."

"Not at all," said Pernic. "I have his report here with me now, though it needs transcribing. That is why we are making a detour on our way to Ancleed. I have an old friend there who can decipher it for us." Tagorin glanced out the port side window. Everything had changed so suddenly. It had been only days ago he and Ilandee were skipping stones across Lake Gray. The abruptness in which all the events had transpired around him left him feeling distant—detached. He had expected a routine trip when he entered Finoval; instead, Ilandee was dead, Dagon was captured and missing, and Tiber had betrayed them. All the while he wondered what Gregory or Vine or the others were do-ing. Did they even know? Tagorin slammed his fist on the table. Enora shot him an annoyed look but said nothing.

"Why did he do it?" asked Tagorin. "We al-ways thought he was one of us."

"You are referring to Tiber?"

"Yes," snarled Tagorin. "He was Ilandee's friend."

"We may never know what Tiber's motives were," said Pernic. "Perhaps, the information Ilan-dee has left us will guide us to the proper an-swers." Silence fell over the cabin once more. The creaks of the ship were eerily loud as the sea rocked the vessel.

"Dedalus was not always the man he is now," said Pernic after some time had passed. "I knew Dedalus well in his youth and traveled long and far with him throughout all of Aldure. He was modest, caring, and deeply interested in the welfare of those who inhabited Aldure. He and a select few were responsible for the very formation of the Band of Kings. One could easily argue he destroyed his own creation.

"Many liked him, including myself. I found his thirst for knowledge intriguing—so much that I often followed in his pursuits. It was his knowledge and skill, for instance, that created the Azura lamps. I once called him friend. No one would have guessed that he would become the king we have today—no one except his father."

"Is Zythan under his control as well?" asked Tagorin.

"Yes," said Pernic heavily. "There are few

places in all of Aldure that had not been touched in some way by his reach for power."

"Why doesn't anyone do anything about it?" asked Tagorin. "Why only now is there a rebellion forming?"

"Because everyone is afraid," said Enora, speaking to the window. "His supporters are far larger in number than those who oppose him. It doesn't matter if they support him with their true allegiance or if it is their fear of death—both make them dangerous to oppose."

"He must be close to dying," said Tagorin after a moment of silence.

"What makes you think that" asked Pernic.

"Well, he must be old by now," said Tagorin. "No one lives forever."

"But fear and power does," said Pernic. "Do you think that no one will take his place once he is gone? Do you think it not possible that those he surrounds himself with will not one day make a fatal discovery that they too could possess all that he does? The problem resides not on Dedalus alone, but the condition of the whole."

"Maybe once he is gone, people will want to go back to the way they were before," said Tagorin. Pernic chuckled, though it was soft and brief.

"Is that a chance you are willing to take?" Pernic asked. "Do you think all those who have witnessed the power and the riches and the respect that Dedalus receives will not take it the moment it is available? What chance do we take that the good man gets the throne, and furthermore, what hope do we have that the good man will remain so?"

It was midday when the ship set anchor in Zythan's market harbor. Ships were directed into various shipping lanes, both coming and going. At one point the shipping lanes were five ships wide. The docks were equally alive with bustling activity. Zythan, according to Pernic, was nearly twice the population of Finoval, with half the space.

"This way," said Pernic, pointing through a small gap of people in front of them. Tagorin squeezed his way past the tightly woven crowd as he fought to keep sight of Pernic. Enora followed at the rear with much less urgency. Pernic weaved in and out of the chaotic market, making his way to the far end of the dock. Once Tagorin emerged from the crowd, Zythan grew into view.

The docks were completely water bound — none touched a shred of dry land, their expanse covering nearly every inch of shallow seawater. Zythan, Tagorin soon discovered, was a towering fortress of stone and marble. Archery towers loomed over the city outskirts at an alarming interval. The walls (rising from the depths of the sea at various points) were eerily smooth and slanted outward toward the sea from which they came. They complemented the island's unnaturally high cliffs perfectly. Beyond the walls and archery towers were monolith structures composed of shapes Tagorin could not comprehend — many defying the forces of nature. From the docks ascended a long, winding set of stone stairs, carved from the very island. As had been the case in Finoval, White Riders stood at the entrance to Zythan.

"Is that your ship, sir?" asked the Rider pointing.

"No," said Pernic. "We are merely passengers of rented transport."

"Will you be responsible for the docking fee?"

"Yes, yes, of course," said Pernic, reaching into his cloak for a small pouch that jingled lightly. Pernic paid the Rider the adequate fee.

"Thank you, sir," said the Rider. "His Majesty appreciates your observant compliance to Imperium regulations."

"I would not aim to displease His Majesty," said Pernic.

"Quite right," said the Rider. "Protocol requires I ask your purpose for your visit today."

"Trade," said Pernic.

"There is adequate commerce on the dock," said the Rider. "All goods are available without gaining entrance into Zythan."

"I am also here to visit an old friend who resides here," said Pernic.

"Very well," said the Rider. "We would ask that your friend take extra care not to draw any weapon while a guest of the city." He gave Enora a stern glare.

"Of course," said Pernic. Enora gave the Rider a brief smile. Apparently satisfied, the Rider stepped aside and allowed them to pass.

Zythan was a palace compared with Finoval. The streets were paved in granite and marble. Each building was unlike the one before; one twisted as

103

it rose toward the sky while another stood perfectly straight and square. Every house or shop was unique and placed on a very apparent grid system, each occupying equal-sized spaces. Only one trait was shared among them: All were made of the same dark, glassy stone.

Despite the harshness of the buildings, Tagorin rather thought Zythan could have been enjoyable. Unlike Finoval, Zythan was pristine and well kept, conveying a sense of royalty or grandeur. He imagined Ilandee as a child, running down the streets with his brothers. The very thought of Ilandee growing up in such a neat and ordered place clashed with the harsh ruffian image he had known all his life.

As Pernic led them down the street, Tagorin noticed how empty the city was apart from the occasional White Rider. Tagorin supposed they were away on the docks. Shops were void of any traffic, many with closed signs hung on their doors.

"Pernic," said Tagorin after some time, "why is Zythan so nice and Finoval is not? Aren't they both under Dedalus's control?

"Zythan is not the only city to have the king's good grace," answered Pernic. "As you know, not all the kings joined Triton's rebellion. Those who willingly bowed at Dedalus's feet were handsomely rewarded. Their cities were left untouched. Finoval is but a shadow of its former self. Zythan, you should know, is home to Dedalus's naval forces. The harbor in which we docked is but one of three shipping docks occupying the island."

They continued down the wide marble street, the Azures notably taller and more prominent than they had been in Finoval. Tagorin noticed the street was gradually growing wider and the shops stretching farther apart. He soon understood why.

Tall and manicured cypress trees had emerged on each side of them, surrounded with flowers of varying types, a rainbow of color at their trunks. They followed the path farther until they entered a large plaza. A two-story statue was anchored at the center, a creature unlike anything Tagorin had ever seen. It had the body of an enormous fish, but its torso and head were that of a man. Around the statue was a pond with a dozen shooting fountains that sprayed water over the creature. Around the fountain were hundreds of tables and tents. Most surprisingly were the dozens of people dressed in green, hustling around tying down tent straps and moving about under a barrage of commands by a single man dressed in the most absurd green uniform Tagorin had ever seen. His shoes were those of fins, and his hat was that of a fish head. Most striking was his coat; it came down as any coat did to the waist, but then it had a long tail at the back, much like the statue's form. His face had been painted green to match the color of his outfit.

"What is going on?" asked Tagorin.

"The Havstrambe," answered Pernic.

"The what?" asked Tagorin.

"It is a celebration," said Pernic, motioning for them to follow as he continued around the plaza. "The Havstrambe was a water demon. It had the body of an enormous fish but the torso and head of a man. The man was said to have long, flowing green hair with a beard to match. It is why everything you see here is green. Every year a celebration is held to show respect to the creature."

"Why?" asked Tagorin further.

"Well, it is a story with many variations," said Pernic. "We shall hear it tonight. But first, we must attend to my old friend." They walked the perimeter of the plaza, careful to avoid any run-ins with the workers, and pursued one of the side streets. Eventually, they came to a modestly sized shop at a dead end. Its windows were very narrow but quite tall. Above a narrow door hung a worn sign that read The Vine.

"This is the place, I believe," said Pernic. He knocked on the door twice and waited. There was a scuffle, the unmistakable sound of crashing porcelain, followed by a short burst of cursing. Then a sequence of unlocking could be heard from behind the door; chains and latches and the like were easily distinguishable. Slowly, the door opened, and a voice floated from within.

"Come in, come in." Tagorin followed behind Pernic and Enora, entering the shop one at a time through narrow door.

"Clifford, it is good to see you, my old friend," said Pernic, greeting the man with a warm embrace. When the two had parted, Tagorin could hardly believe his eyes.

"Vine?" asked Tagorin, staring at the old man as he hunched over his short cane. Enora, confused, looked between the two.

"You know each other?" asked Enora, her eyebrows raised.

"I don't understand," said Tagorin quickly. "I thought, but you were with—"

"Patience, Tagorin," said Pernic. "All will

be explained. Clifford, might we intrude upon your hospitality for a while?"

"This way," said Vine, ushering them from the entryway. The shop was dimly lit, and the air was thick with dust. Enora was quick to comment.

"Has anyone ever cleaned this place?" she choked out.

"Beg your pardon, madam," said Vine as he led them down the hall. "I only returned here yesterday."

"This is your place, Vine?" asked Tagorin, who was also finding it hard to speak with the dust.

"Oh yes," said Vine. "Only I've been away for a long time. Come, the room to the right is a bit more open." Everything was cluttered. Books and strewn papers with dust coatings were stacked in the corners of the room as high as the door. The table in the center was buried beneath drawings of various ships and parts and random figures Tagorin had never seen before. The chairs accompanying the table were burdened with various mechanical parts or rags or other miscellaneous items.

"Make yourselves at home," said Vine. "I'll put on some tea." He walked to the far end of the room and rummaged through a cupboard. A few moments later, Vine emerged from the cupboard with a severely dusty teapot. Tagorin glanced at Enora, who wore a disgusted look. Pernic, however, appeared quite calm and relaxed. He took a chair, moved its contents elsewhere, shook off the gathered dust, and made himself comfortable.

"It has been a long time since my last visit," said Pernic, his eyes dancing around the walls of the shop with interest. He pointed to a drawing that hung high on the wall nearest a window. "That ship is the standard vessel used by the navy here on the island." He smiled and continued to observe the room while Tagorin and Enora stood, unsure what to do. Neither wanted to touch anything.

"Going to stand, then?" asked Vine as he returned to the room with a tray of cups and pot of tea (no longer dusty). He asked Pernic if he would clear a place, to which Pernic happily obliged. When Vine had set the table, he went to the chairs around the table and simply tipped them over one by one, tossing their contents to the dusty floor. He did not bother relocating any of the displaced items but instead sat in the chair nearest to Pernic and poured the tea. Exchanging looks of disgust, Tagorin and Enora took their seats. Enora, Tagorin noticed, sat at the very edge of her seat.

"I believe introductions are in order," said Pernic. "You know Tagorin already, of course." Vine nodded in response.

"This lovely young lady before you," continued Pernic with a grand gesture, "is Enora."

"Pleased to meet you, my dear," said Vine, bowing. He took a sip of his tea and turned his attention to Tagorin.

"Am I to assume Ilandee never made it?" he asked. Tagorin had not expected this question so soon. He opened his mouth to respond but could not force any words.

"Ilandee has passed on," said Pernic, placing a hand on Tagorin's shoulder. "I have had his body brought with us on the ship. We will be taking him to Ancleed to be buried with his brothers."

"Only fitting," said Vine. He again turned

his attention to Tagorin. "What of Dagon?"

"Captured," interjected Pernic once more. "Ortho has him. Ilandee attempted to rescue the boy."

"I see," said Vine, taking another sip of his tea. "And I presume you have the parcel?"

"Yes," said Pernic, reaching into his cloak and handing the parcel to Vine. "I would assume Ilandee sent you here ahead on the chances of his death." Vine only nodded, as his eyes darted back and forth over the parchment. He then hobbled over to the same cupboard he had fetched the teapot from earlier, pulling out this time a dusty black strongbox. He reached into his pants pocket and pulled from them a ring of miscellaneous keys and observed each one in passing. Then, after a dozen or so keys, he took one and unlocked the box before him. Tagorin was rather surprised to find only more paper inside.

"Ilandee knew we were being watched," said Vine as he went through the papers one by one. "Ilandee likewise knew Felix and the king were setting a trap for him. He didn't tell me the contents of this letter, but that I'd be the one decoding it in the event he didn't make it to Zythan with you." Vine continued through his pile of papers. Tagorin found it hard to focus. How much had he been kept in the dark?

"Vine," asked Tagorin, "how come no one told me, you know, about all this?"

"Tagorin," responded Vine, "you must understand Ilandee had no desire to keep anything from you. The less you knew, the safer you were." He paused and looked directly into Tagorin's eyes. Tagorin had never noticed before how old Vine truly was until now. Every line in his face was prevalent and proud. "More than anything, Ilandee wanted you safe. You were like a son to him—both of you were."

"You will have answers soon, Tagorin," said Pernic. "For now, you must be patient and let Clifford see to his work." Vine continued through his stack of papers for what must have been the next hour before shouting something no one could comprehend.

"I've found it," said Vine, his voice returning to normal. "I've found the transcription key. This must be very important information indeed for Ilandee to use such archaic language."

"Explain," said Pernic.

"Simple," said Vine. "This alphabet belonged to our ancestors. It is the language that preceded the Old Way."

"Marvelous," said Pernic, gazing at the letter. He stared for a moment then pointed at one of the shapes. "I see the resemblance now. I am rather surprised I did not notice this myself."

"Give me a moment," said Vine, taking out a fresh leaf of parchment and a quill. Line by line, Vine transcribed the letter. By the time Vine had finished, they had all been through two additional pots of tea and the daylight had all but expired.

"Here it is," said Vine, handing the new letter to Pernic. Pernic read through the letter to himself and then cleared his throat and read aloud.

If you are reading this letter, it means that I have fallen victim to the trap laid before me. I have included in this report the most complete map of the White Rider

Order resupply routes as well as the volume associated with those routes, with detailed ledgers. Perhaps this will help turn the tide for Triton and those committed to the cause.

But that is the end of my happy report. The move of the White Rider Order was more than political convenience for the king; it would have been very easy to find a replacement for the overseer. The king is moving the Order there firstly because there have been recent protests in the city. And it is the nature of those protests that has caused the king's hand in such a hostile manner. Many are calling for his dethronement, but it goes beyond this; my sources inside the city of Zythan have confirmed order for a fleet of ships to be built and sent to dock in Finoval, which has never had its own naval force. He is preparing for an assault in the northeast — likely Ancleed. Finoval provides the best launching port for his White Riders — it will be far more efficient for him to send his army by ship than it will be to send them through the Hackastines and the Field of Tears that follow. The king is well aware of the opposition building against him in the east. Ancleed must be prepared for the battle. It is my suspicion they will attack within the coming months before winter hits.

Pernic finished reading the letter and turned his attention to the other documentation.

"Can you have this sent to the right people?" asked Pernic.

"Of course," said Vine. "I have a contact who reports directly to the Jarl."

"Excellent. Has construction of the ships Ilandee mentioned begun yet?"

"Yes," said Vine. "The informant he spoke of is

none other than myself. Twenty frigates are under construction and will be completed within a few months. They've been at it for some time. They'll carry up to five thousand troops and White Riders combined."

"Then we are without much time."

"You'll be needing a ship," said Vine. "I can have one ready to leave just before daybreak. I can have Ilandee's body transferred as well."

"Thank you," said Pernic.

"Unfortunately, it does not come free."

"Is it with crew?" asked Pernic.

"For a price," said Vine. His right leg bounced up and down now as he eyed Pernic with consideration.

"Very well," said Pernic, pulling out a modest coin purse from his robes. "How much?"

"You have to pay the docking fee, of course," said Vine.

"How much?" asked Pernic again.

"And the crew," continued Vine as though he hadn't heard Pernic at all.

"How much, Clifford?"

"One hundred and fifty sovereigns for the ship and crew. You pay the docking fees when you depart."

"Very well," said Pernic. "One hundred and fifty minus the fifty you still owe me from that joint venture five years ago."

"Times are hard," said Vine. "I have to start from nothing again."

"You know the king's policy on owed debt, Clifford," said Pernic.

"Empty threat, Pernic," said Vine.

"How do you know my opinion has not changed these last five years?"

"Fee's the same," said Vine stubbornly. "I'd be crackers to believe what you just said." Pernic shook his head and began counting out (to Tagorin's horror) slowly and deliberately each of the one hundred and fifty sovereigns. When Pernic had finished, the purse was nearly empty.

"This will be used well," said Vine, scooping up the sovereigns. Pernic stood and walked himself to the door. Tagorin and Enora rushed to follow him.

"That was disgusting," said Enora as she beat dust from her clothes.

"He's always been a bit messy," said Tagorin.

"He has lived a difficult life," said Pernic.

"So he can't clean up a bit?" asked Enora. Pernic shook his head with a chuckle, and together the three of them walked down the street toward the night's celebration.

CHAPTER ELEVEN: THE HAVSTRAMBE

The plaza was alive with dancing and music; marching drums and bagpipes erupted in song as a dozen green-clothed men danced around the plaza perimeter. Jugglers went from table to table scavenging any item their patrons would part with, promising a grand display of skill. Tables upon tables had been lined with food the likes of which Tagorin had never seen. As expected, the plaza was bathed in light from the Azuras.

"This way," said Pernic, his voice just audible over the music. Pernic weaved himself through the crowd while Tagorin and Enora scrambled to keep his pace. Near the end of the first table they found Pernic, sitting with a pipe already in hand, deep in conversation with another spectator.

"Sit, sit," said Pernic hurriedly. He waved his free hand with enthusiasm. The dancers had made their way to the center of the plaza, each holding what appeared to Tagorin as a portable version of the Azura. Turning his attention to the table, he found it burdened with food and wine. Dozens of baskets of fresh-baked breads, rolls, and biscuits were lined down the center of the table, accompanied by jellies and jams of any fruit imaginable. Flagons of wine were passed down the table, each patron pouring his or her own. Platters of meats were also prominent. Tagorin did not know where to begin.

Tagorin turned to Enora, who, surprisingly, returned a brief smile as she took from one of the breadbaskets.

"So, how long have you known Pernic?" asked Tagorin.

"Most of my life," said Enora. "He is like a grandfather to me."

"You're an orphan?"

"Yes," said Enora, her expression now slightly saddened. "My parents were killed in the rebellion."

"I'm sorry," said Tagorin. He had not expected her answer.

"It's all right," she said. "Pernic has taken good care of me." And with that, she gave Tagorin another smile before biting into her bread. The drums grew louder, and Tagorin could feel the pulse beat on his chest. Gradually the bagpipes began to fade as the crescendo of cadence turned into a primal thunder. The dancers accelerated their steps, circling the center statue in a near daze. The tension of the drums and dancers continued to build until quite abruptly, they stopped. The man Tagorin had witnessed earlier barking orders during the festival setup had emerged from among the dancers. His fish costume glowed an eerie green in the Azura light.

"Centuries ago, the waters were violent and cruel," the young man recited. His voice was low and crisp. "The sea was a dangerous place for man and beast alike. Our strongest ships were strewn and tossed by the rogue waves of the untamed oceans. The waters were not to be ruled by man.

"The waters could not be tamed by man, for within them raged a war more destructive than man had ever seen. Vile and hideous sea serpents swam the swiftest currents, denying sea vessels safe passage to newer lands. Gigantic and repulsive creatures from the deep controlled the will of the water, ensuring that no man could hope to conquer it. Man was destined to live by land and land alone, forever an outcast to the mysteries of the sea.

"Among all the wicked beasts of the untamed sea was the lord of the waters himself, Hakenmann, half fish and half man and as long as a brigantine. He commanded all the sea beasts under harsh whip, and they did his bidding. He would not allow man to sail in his waters." The young man began to pace now, moving from table to table, making eye contact with all he could.

"Hakenmann had a brother," the man continued, "a kind and gentle creature. He too was half fish and half man. Havstrambe was his name, friend to man and land-beast alike. Havstrambe challenged his brother to a great sea battle. The stakes were high: the rule of the sea and all its creatures and their very lives. Nine days a storm raged on the open water, hurricanes hit the shores, and typhoons erupted around them. Tidal waves taller than any sailor dare claim to have seen struck Aldure with a crash louder than thunder. The sea in which they fought to command threatened to consume their very souls.

"On the ninth day a tidal wave rose above them, tired of the chaos and an empty throne. The sea threatened to take its own command. Havstrambe pulled away from the death grip of Hakenmann, who was not so fortunate. The wave twisted around his enormous body, pulling him down with a whirlpool that led to the depths where no creature lived.

"But Havstrambe could not bear to see his brother departed. With the rage of a typhoon, Havstrambe leaped into the whirlpool, swimming with all his might against the raging current after his brother. The sea turned its gaze and fury to Havstrambe, hoping to claim yet another.

"But Havstrambe was the true master of the sea; he reached to his brother and carried him on his back to safety and away from the cold waves of the sea. The sea grew furious and sent all his monsters in pursuit. But Havstrambe was master of the sea, and he bade them to stop—and they did. He bade them to swim his brother to the shore of Aldure. Alone, Havstrambe would settle the score. Havstrambe bellowed to the darkness of the sea and commanded it to yield. The sea laughed and drowned him in a furious tidal wave. But Havstrambe was master of the sea, and so the wave could not drown him. Havstrambe swam the height of the next wave until he could see all; from there on the crest of the wave he bellowed once more, 'I am Havstrambe, master of the sea, and you bend to my command.' And the sea was forced to obey the might of his voice. To this day, Havstrambe keeps the sea at bay. When storms rage at sea, you can rest assured Havstrambe will calm them once more." The young storyteller bowed, and the crowd erupted in cheer as the bagpipes and drums and dancers commenced a second time.

"There is more to come," said Pernic.

The music halted a second time, and with it three of the dancers stepped forward. They were dressed as Havstrambe and Hakenmann, with the

117

third attempting to dress as the ocean. It was a silent performance, though it was clearly a reenactment of the great battle. Most of the crowd awed or cheered at the right places, (even when the dancer posing as the ocean tripped over Havstrambe).

All through the night, jugglers juggled and dancers danced as the inhabitants of Zythan ate and drank to their hearts' content. Pernic had somehow interjected himself into a conversation between two older gentlemen about proper taxation while Enora remained content with watching the dancers. Tagorin found his mind wandering.

It was hard for him to grasp his situation; Ilandee was dead and stored in a cargo hold of a ship while the entire city of Zythan celebrated. Miles away, another city had been attacked from within. Ships for war were being built, and yet, the people around him lived as though nothing were wrong. Among all these thoughts, he wondered desperately where Dagon had been taken prisoner — or if he were still alive. These thoughts continued to occupy Tagorin's mind even as he followed Pernic and Enora to an inn when the celebrations had concluded. He was hardly aware of being led to his room.

"We have an early rise tomorrow," said Pernic. "I shall fetch you when it is time." Tagorin nodded and closed the door to his room. It was small but cozy. A small window rested just above the head of his bed. With his thoughts still on Dagon, he crawled into bed.

CHAPTER TWELVE: ENORA'S BURDEN

Yuck," shouted Enora as she toed down the stairs of the ship's cabin. They were coated in dust. Pernic could be heard chuckling behind them. The cabin was far smaller than the ship they had arrived in; a few bunked beds lined each side of the room, and a large rectangular table stood in the middle surrounded by chairs. Toward the back of the cabin was a single window with a view from the rear of the ship. A few barrels rested just below the windowsill.

"The blankets are dusty," said Enora, prodding one of the blankets. The dust rose into the air, each particle sparkling in the window light. "I'm not sleeping in these." Pernic chose not to respond but instead swept dust from one of the chairs and sat down facing the rear window. Tagorin set his newly acquired pack down by one of the beds and sat in the chair opposite of Pernic. Enora continued to stare at the beds.

"You can stop worrying about the beds, Enora," said Pernic. "We will arrive in Ancleed before the sun sets." Enora gave a sigh of relief and joined them at the table.

"What is Ancleed like?" asked Tagorin.

"It is far different from Finoval or Zythan," said Pernic. "During the rebellion, most of the city was destroyed by Dedalus and his army. It was only a year or so ago that Triton reclaimed the city."

"Is Triton there now?" asked Tagorin.

"Yes," said Pernic. "He is expecting us."

"You said something about burying Ilandee

next to his brothers."

"I did."

"Who were they?" he asked. "Ilandee never said anything about having brothers."

"Well," said Pernic, "I told you earlier that Ilandee came from royal blood, yes?" Tagorin nodded. "And so he did. Ilandee's father, Ademus, served on the Magistrate under King Alexander, before the Band of Kings had ever been established. Ilandee's father died of old age in service to the crown. When the Band of Kings was first being formed, King Alexander did not forget Ademus's service. He appointed Ilandee's elder brother, Naborus, to the throne of Ancleed. He also appointed Ilandee's younger brother, Cadmus, to the throne of Zythan."

"Why wasn't Ilandee offered?" asked Tagorin.

"He refused," said Pernic. "He was later convinced to serve as an ambassador for King Alexander." Tagorin peered from the cabin window, watching until the docks of Zythan had vanished from view. They sat in silence for a considerable time, the only noise coming from the creaks of the ship and the chopping of water against the vessel.

"How did your parents die?" asked Tagorin after some time. Enora didn't respond immediately. She gave a quick look to Pernic, who assured her with a deliberate nod.

"They were murdered," she said, her voice barely audible.

"By whom?"

"Dedalus," she said, her voice quieter still.

"Did you know your parents?"

"I need some air," said Enora, standing so abruptly she shook the table. She excused herself and climbed the cabin stairs to the ship's deck.

"I didn't mean to upset her," said Tagorin.

"She will come around," said Pernic. "Like you, she too has experienced a life without a family, a family she cannot remember. And she carries an immense responsibility the two of us can hardly fathom."

"What do you mean?" asked Tagorin.

"King Alexander had two wives in the course of his life. His first wife, Celine, died of a terrible sickness, not long after giving birth to her son, Dedalus. King Alexander lived many years without seeking another wife, despite the counseling of his advisers. When Dedalus had neared the age of eighteen, King Alexander found himself attracted to another woman and was soon married again.

"Elizabeth was a beautiful woman and had a certain stubbornness that made most men...uncomfortable. She was from a small town not far outside Ancleed. This woman is Enora's mother."

"Wait," said Tagorin as a dawning comprehension fell over him. "Are you saying—that Enora—that she is a princess?"

"Queen," Pernic corrected. "The rightful heir to the Grand Thone."

"Wow," said Tagorin. He began imagining Enora in royal dresses, laden with gold and precious gems. He found himself immersed in a completely changed Enora, an Enora he would never have imagined.

"She does not envy it," said Pernic, breaking Tagorin from his thoughts.

"But why?" asked Tagorin. "Wouldn't she prefer to be Queen of Aldure rather than let Dedalus remain as king?"

"And that is why she will fight to take her place at the Grand Throne," said Pernic. "Not because it is her desire, but because it is her responsibility. She has seen the suffering of her people, and she has suffered the same injustices and cruelties as her people. She has decided to stand against Dedalus, and in doing so, she, like many others, risks her life to see a better future. She will have many responsibilities in the coming months, responsibilities, Tagorin, that are not to be coveted or idolized." Tagorin found himself unable to speak. Now, he felt incredibly foolish.

"As I said earlier," said Pernic, his solemn expression turned cheerful again, "she will come around. She is brash, and sometimes hotheaded, but very forgiving."

"Will there really be another war?" asked Tagorin.

"Yes," said Pernic. "You recall Ilandee's letter? You saw the ships in the harbor — did they look like cargo ships to you? The first battle will assuredly begin in Ancleed, where the first rebellion ended." Tagorin immediately imagined the field of combat; knights and soldiers battling with swords and spears while arrows flew overhead. It was also at this moment Tagorin realized his own reservations. He found himself staring into his hands.

"I see you appreciate the severity of the situation," said Pernic after a while. "When the time comes, what will you do, Tagorin?"

"I just want to save my friend," said Tagorin.

"I don't want to fight a war."

"I told you before," said Pernic gravely, "that to save your friend you would face the king and his army."

"I've never been in a war," argued Tagorin. "I don't know how to fight."

"When the time comes," said Pernic, his gaze returning to the window, "we will all find ourselves in the midst of our greatest struggles — our greatest battle — and it is there we will find our true selves." He turned to Tagorin, placing a hand on his shoulder.

"That time is fast approaching, and we will rise to the challenge."

CHAPTER THIRTEEN: WELCOMING PARTY

The rest of the ship ride had been under strained silence. Tagorin, embarrassed from his encounter with Enora, had not said another word. Pernic had attempted to lighten the mood with one of his stories, but neither Tagorin nor Enora tried very hard to listen. When the ship had docked in Ancleed, it was well into the early hours of nightfall.

They were not allowed to leave the ship, however. Pernic explained that because they had come from territory controlled by Dedalus, a thorough search had to be conducted, and each of them would be detained and questioned on board until receiving the necessary clearance.

Four Ancleed soldiers entered the ship's cabin, two of whom stood guard at the doorway with spears at the ready and their free hands upon the hilts of their swords. They were easily distinguishable from the White Riders Tagorin had become accustomed to seeing. The soldiers were equipped with steel helms and chest plates, underneath which they wore red garments that were accompanied with leather padding in places where traditional armor had not been available. The remaining two soldiers took Pernic by the arms to the deck of the ship, leaving Tagorin and Enora alone.

"I'm sorry," said Tagorin, his voice just above a whisper. "I didn't mean to upset you earlier." Enora did not respond verbally, but she nodded all the same. Their guards remained stationary and motionless. Time passed slowly. Tagorin wondered what had happened to Pernic.

"Do you think he'll be all right?" asked Tagorin.

"He usually is," said Enora.

"He's really old," said Tagorin. "He can't defend himself."

"Stop talking, you two," said one of the guards. He pointed his spear at them. "Remain quiet unless you've been addressed." Not wanting to upset the guards further, the two fell silent. Tagorin tried to distract his mind by counting the wood grains in the table, but he lost count several times. Then after a long while, they heard steps above and soon after coming down the cabin stairs.

At the front, his face beaming, Pernic led his new company into the cabin. He then stood to the side. His free arm and staff gestured toward Tagorin and Enora. The same two guards who had taken Pernic topside entered first, taking their places beside the other two guards. Then, a much shorter figure entered the cabin.

He was but an inch or so taller than Tagorin, but his dress and stature were that of royalty. He stood with a rigid poise, his arms at his sides. His robes, red in color and trimmed with the faintest hint of gold, swept the cabin floor. A hood and a graying black beard hid the man's face. He approached a few steps closer to the table, where Enora and Tagorin were still seated. And then the most unexpected thing happened.

The man fell to his knees and removed the hood from his face. A silver-and-gold crown sat upon his curly peppered black hair. His emerald eyes hovered briefly over Tagorin and settled upon Enora. The guards followed the strange man's actions, falling to their knees and lowering their heads. Tagorin turned to Pernic, and saw that he too had taken a knee. Tagorin then looked to Enora, whose gaze he saw fell upon the crowned man before her.

"My humble apologies," said the man, his eyes now diverted to the floor. "Ancleed welcomes your presence, milady." He then stood and took a moment to regain his composure. "I am Triton, once Jarl of Finoval and loyal to the late King Alexander, your father. We welcome your presence here in Ancleed."

"Thank you," said Enora, her response polite but noticeably unsteady.

"Come," said the Jarl, taking Enora in a one-armed embrace. "We have prepared accommodations in the old Avar Castle for you and your company." Tagorin watched as they and the guards exited the cabin, leaving Pernic and Tagorin quite alone.

"Come, Tagorin," said Pernic. "We are also expected."

The reception was unbelievable. The docks had been crowded to their fullest extent with curious and anxious citizens. When Triton had announced Enora's arrival, the whole city of Ancleed had come alive with cheers and chants, their voices deafening. Two horse-drawn stagecoaches awaited them.

Enora and Triton had been sent ahead on the first, while Tagorin and Pernic were ushered into the second.

Within minutes, they had arrived at Avar Castle, which Pernic informed Tagorin had been almost entirely rebuilt from its nearly complete destruction after the rebellion.

"This is where Ilandee's older brother had lived and ruled the city of Ancleed." Tagorin found in himself a renewed sense of excitement for the first time since leaving Finoval.

The grand foyer was monolithic—easily a hundred feet wide and twice as long. Tall stone columns reached multiple stories, each with detailed carvings and etchings of various images ranging from battle depictions to ornate shapes. The floor was made of polished color-swirling marble that reflected brilliant arrays of blues, reds, and golds. A red carpet traveled the length of the foyer, leading to a raised platform where three decorated chairs stood elevated above the hall. Behind the platform two large banners were draped on the wall. One was a coat of arms; a simple shield with the Avar name, accompanied with swords on each side. Beneath the shield read the motto *Courage will lead the heart true*. The second banner was identical to the one Tagorin had seen in the summit temple of the Hackastine Pass. This banner was pristine and full of color. The silver tree glistened magnificently, and the purple of the banner was deep and dark.

As they made their way toward the thrones of the castle, they were cheered yet further by its keepers and servants of the castle. Enora was seated first in the middle throne, followed by Triton at her right. Pernic was given the third seat, while Tagorin stood at the foot of the platform. Gradually, the cheering and clapping faded, and Triton stood.

"Citizens of Aldure, and citizens of Ancleed, today is a joyous day," said Triton, his voice surprisingly booming. "Today, our future begins. Today, we begin to rewrite history. Today, in the dark hours of the morning, we begin celebration of a new dawn—a new future. Today, we begin the end of tyranny." The Jarl paused as the castle erupted in applause and cheering.

"It is with great pleasure—and honor—that I present to you, the daughter of the late King Alexander, heir of the Grand Throne, and queen of Aldure, Enora." The crowd cheered its loudest yet, falling to their knees in a grand wave. Triton then urged Enora to step forward.

"Address your people, Your Highness."

"I do not know what to say," said Enora, glancing nervously to Pernic. Pernic gave her an encouraging smile.

"Tell only what speaks most on your heart," said Pernic. "Do this with sincerity and conviction, and your people will stand behind you." She stood then, for a moment her expression unreadable. She was not clothed in the royal garments or adorned with crown, yet somehow unexplainable to Tagorin, she stood before all of Ancleed confident.

"I don't know how to be a queen," said Enora, her voice quiet but clear. "I have never acted a single day with the responsibilities of an entire people on my shoulders. And I will never be able to replace my father." She glanced again to Pernic, who, still smiling, nodded to her encouragingly.

"But I share in your pain," Enora continued, her voice a bit stronger. "Like you, I have lived under the chains of a tyrant too long. Like you, I yearn to be free. This I promise to you: I will fight for you and for the freedom of Aldure once more." The castle rang with a thunderous cheer. All throughout the crowd, words unmistakable by any rang out:

Long live Queen Enora.

CHAPTER FOURTEEN: BURIAL

The next week passed at Avar Castle, and not once had Tagorin caught sight of Enora or the Jarl since the arrival ceremony (apart from dinner, in which case he was not important enough to hold company with the princess). Equally busy, Pernic had come around to check on Tagorin only when he had a moment to spare. Nonetheless, Pernic had made it a point to inform him that Ilandee's funeral service was to be held that afternoon.

Still, the week had been eventful. Tagorin found himself wandering the castle corridors and exploring whatever rooms were made available to him. He had been explicitly told not to venture into the west wing. Aside from the momentary feeling of abandonment by Pernic, Tagorin welcomed the solitude and the freedom to walk about. Often, he passed many workers who were in a hurry to complete last-minute repairs on the castle. Occasionally, he would stop and ask them questions, but they were rarely any help.

Avar Castle was built in a quadrant fashion, with the grand foyer as the center and a wing in each of the cardinal directions. The north wing was the least interesting and smallest of all the wings. It contained the castle kitchen, pantry, and bathing room. The south wing had been Tagorin's favorite so far, containing a vast library, a multitude of guest rooms (one of which had been prepared for Tagorin), and a spiraling tower that overlooked the entire city of Ancleed. It was here that Tagorin spent most of his time. Pernic had requested that he not leave the castle without him (which Tagorin now believed would be an eternity).

Ancleed stretched for miles, lining the coast and reaching north over rolling hills. Despite its expanse, Ancleed was noticeably empty. Conquered first by war, Ancleed was a ruin taken over by desertion and nature. The impacts of war had not been erased over time. Buildings of various heights were crumbled and broken, and others simply toppled. But Ancleed was not dead—not yet. As the days passed, Tagorin noticed from the tower window pockets of resilience. Near the castle was a market, busy with flocks of people. Near the docks, new shops and ship assemblies were reborn, one bit of scaffolding at a time.

The east wing was available for Tagorin to explore, but like the north wing, it did not offer much for his curiosity. It had been the royal chambers of Naborus (Ilandee's older brother). One worker had told him the east wing had been destroyed during Dedalus's siege and had been restored only a month before their arrival. Despite all the work that had been done, Tagorin had yet to find anything of the family that had once resided in the castle.

Precisely an hour past noon, Tagorin was interrupted from his window gazing.

"I can recall the numerous conversations I once had with Ilandee in this very spot," said Pernic, emerging from the stairwell. As usual, he held his unlit pipe in his right hand and his staff in his left. He joined Tagorin at the tower window, his gaze not on the city but the sea and hills beyond. After some time, Pernic pointed past the rolling hills and the far reaches of Ancleed.

"Beyond those hills is a place called the Field of Tears," said Pernic. "It has been the place of many battles, but none so gruesome as the one that took the lives of Naborus and the brave men and women who stood before Dedalus."

"Why do they bother?" asked Tagorin, his eyes sweeping over Ancleed. "Don't they know it will all be destroyed again?"

"Perhaps," said Pernic. "But that is not the point, is it?" Tagorin looked at Pernic. He had lit his pipe now, his gaze still toward the rolling hills.

"We know neither the day nor the hour of our end, but it does not stop us from hoping and trusting in a better future. Perhaps they do labor in vain, but it is not worthless. They are not simply rebuilding Ancleed, but rather, they are rebuilding themselves." Pernic exhaled a cloud of smoke. "In the end, it will matter little if nothing remains, so long as we are free."

Ilandee was to be buried next to his brothers in the courtyard inside the castle grounds. It was the first time in a week that Tagorin had stepped out into fresh air. The service had been kept small, according to Pernic, because most who had known Ilandee best were already gone. Vine had made a surprising visit, greeting Tagorin in the most cheerful way he could muster.

"Good to see you, lad," said Vine, shaking

Tagorin's hand. He addressed Pernic in a similar fashion. Aside from Vine, those present for Ilandee's funeral were Enora, Jarl Triton, a few guards (likely there for protection more than Ilandee), and a few faces Tagorin did not know. Vine was quick to pick up on this.

"You see that man next to the Jarl? The one dressed with the hideous overcoat? He is the rebellion's largest financial backer, Seamus Berthog. He runs the banks in Hoethra. And you see the woman next to Princess Enora? She once tried to court Ilandee. Name's Annabel, and believe it or not, she's second in command of the rebellion forces."

It was nearly two o'clock when the services began. They were led through the central courtyard, which extended into a small grove where all the Avar family had been laid to rest. The grove was safely tucked within the curtain walls of the castle, with a single gate facing the sea. A guard stood beside it, his expression bored. The casket (already sealed) had been in place as if waiting for them next to a freshly dug hole. Gradually, the small party surrounded the casket. Triton positioned himself at its head.

"Today, we lay to rest Ilandee Avar," said the Jarl, his voice somber. "Ilandee believed in the freedom of all, and he fought relentlessly to achieve that freedom. He was loyal to both friend and family. Let us never forget that which he fought and died for. Let us remember Ilandee Avar in the coming days when we are faced with our greatest challenges, and let our courage be that which is worthy of the deeds of those who have gone before us and laid the path soundly." Here the Jarl paused a moment. Tagorin turned his gaze from the casket to the king. His eyes were watery, and his fists were clenched. Tagorin looked from one guest to the next, surprised to find nearly all who were present were silently weeping. Vine had fallen to his knees, his sobs the only audible ones. Tagorin too was finding it hard to repress the tears developing in his eyes. He glanced toward Enora, who met his gaze. He hurriedly brushed his tears aside with the sleeve of his shirt. A cold sea wind washed over them as the king gave his closing remarks.

They buried Ilandee between Naborus and Cadmus, his brothers. Pernic had explained that Naborus's grave was actually empty, his body never having been recovered from the Field of Tears. One by one, each of the guests took a turn addressing the gravesite. Tagorin did not approach the freshly engraved tombstone. Instead he watched from a small distance. Gradually, the guests left the grove, few taking any notice of Tagorin. The king, however, approached Tagorin unexpectedly. Tagorin made a quick gesture to go to his knee, but the Jarl caught him and held him by the shoulders.

"He was a good man," said the Jarl, his peppered beard but an inch from Tagorin's face. "Now you must carry on what he started." And then as suddenly as he had approached, he left Tagorin alone. Enora did not address him, but she paused briefly in her walk and gave him a gentle touch on the shoulder. She too left quickly, trailing the king. The banker and the woman named Annabel were next to leave, followed by the king's guard, leaving just Vine, Pernic, and himself in the grove. Vine talked with Pernic in rushed whispers, none of which Tagorin could make out. The cold sea wind washed over them a second time.

Tagorin approached Ilandee's tombstone and fell to his knees. It read simply:

Ilandee Avar
Courage will lead the heart true

CHAPTER FIFTEEN: THE LIFE OF A SOLDIER

Twice, Pernic tried to coax Tagorin from his bed over the next few days, though unsuccessfully. Tagorin had taken to eating his meals in his room, avoiding the busyness of the grand foyer. He was vaguely aware of the castle's ramped-up preparations for the approaching invasion, catching words or phrases by passing guards. He knew, for instance, that Triton had garrisoned roughly four thousand troops in Ancleed, all in preparation for the White Rider invasion. He wanted nothing to do with any of it.

He was also sure Enora had forgotten all about him — why wouldn't she, after all? She was a queen now. Vine had returned to Zythan upon the conclusion of the funeral. Indeed, despite Triton's grand words of remembrance, the castle felt as if it had moved on without Ilandee. Tagorin had never felt so alone. His thoughts would shift from Ilandee to Dagon. Amid all of Pernic's insistences, he could not see how this ragtag band of guards and rebels had anything to do with Dagon's rescue. It made him more than alone — he felt trapped.

On the third night after Ilandee's burial, Tagorin (having forgotten to close his door from his solitary trip to the kitchens) heard a huddle of voices near his room.

"Am I to understand, that you have yet to tell the boy?" Tagorin recognized the voice almost immediately. It was the Jarl's.

"No," said Pernic. "The time is not right."

"He deserves to know, Pernic," said the Jarl.

"You can't keep this from him forever."

"I have already given you my stance," said Pernic, his voice slightly on edge.

"I am sympathetic to the boy," said the Jarl, "and your concern is equally noted, but when, Pernic, do you plan to tell him?"

"Soon," said Pernic.

"I agree with the Jarl," said Enora. Tagorin felt his heart skip a beat. "Tagorin should be told, sooner rather than later."

"I will not discuss this any further," said Pernic.

"What of the traitor, then?" asked the Jarl. "I've had three reports come to my attention today, all claiming that Tiber is indeed in the city." Tagorin felt his heart skip a second time.

"Leave him for now," said Pernic. "Keep a close eye on him; his presence here can mean only one thing. The less the castle knows about Tagorin, the safer he is."

"Very well," said the Jarl.

"Have you any news from Vine?" asked Pernic.

"Yes," responded the Jarl. "The ships will be fully constructed and seaworthy within a couple weeks. It will still take some time for them to load the necessary supplies, but the time is quickly approaching." Tagorin waited to hear more, but they had moved on down the hall. Tagorin could feel his heart pounding in his chest. Tiber was in Ancleed.

He lay awake that night, contemplating how he would escape the castle. Pernic had made it clear he was not to leave. The main doors of the foyer were always guarded by at least two soldiers, if not more. Tagorin knew they would not let him pass. He also knew from his late-night strolls to the kitchens that soldiers were so frequent in the halls that he would never slip through undetected. Thoughts of escape filled his mind until he fell asleep.

Tagorin woke the following morning to two soldiers barging into his room. Without introduction or so much as a word, they dumped a heavy pile consisting of clothing, metal, and a sword onto his bed.

"What's this?" asked Tagorin, not fully awake.

"You're new attire, lad," said one of the soldiers.

"These look like a soldier's garments," said Tagorin.

"Sharp," said the soldier. "You're one of us."

"I'm not a soldier," protested Tagorin.

"Fine," said the soldier, already on his way out, "a dead man, then." The other solider laughed and followed behind, leaving Tagorin alone. Shortly afterward, Pernic and, surprisingly, Triton entered his room, both serious in expression.

"The Jarl and I believe it to be in your best interest that you be trained in arms," said Pernic immediately. "You will work daily with one of the Jarl's sergeants until your skills are adequate for confrontation."

"I've never been in battle before," said Tagorin. "And what difference can I possibly make in this situation?"

"One man can turn the tide of battle at any moment," said the Jarl. "And while it may not be you who leads the tide, you will still earn your keep in this castle. Secondly, Pernic has discussed with me the situation of your friend. You can't expect my men to risk their lives for something you yourself would not do. At any rate, any man should be ready to defend himself when the need arises. My sergeant will meet you at the barracks today at a quarter past noon. Don't be late." The Jarl withdrew himself, leaving Pernic and Tagorin to themselves.

"I told you that to save your friend, you would be facing the king and his forces. I cannot help you unless you acquire the necessary skills to save your friend. I shall wait for you at the castle entrance." Pernic then excused himself, leaving Tagorin to change into his new wardrobe.

That same hour, Tagorin navigated the halls of the castle, passing both soldiers and laborers dashing back and forth from one end of the castle to another. Pernic was waiting as he said he would, leaning on his wooden staff.

"This way," said Pernic, leading him to the castle doors. Pernic nodded to the guards stationed on each side, and they responded in kind, opening the doors to the courtyard.

"Where are we going?" asked Tagorin.

"To the barracks," said Pernic. "Did you already forget the Jarl's instructions?"

"No, it's just early, isn't it?"

"Best to be early than on time or, worse, late," said Pernic. The courtyard was, if anything, more hectic than the castle interior. Carts loaded with hewn stone were scattered up and along the fortification walls. The sounds of carpenters' saws, masons' chisels, and grinding wheels echoed throughout the courtyard. Louder still was the voice of the quartermaster at a nearby tent as he issued supplies to what appeared to be new recruits.

The barracks had been located near the portcullis gate that linked the inner and outer wards together. It was a considerable building, three stories taller than the inner-ward walls and easily twice the width of the castle kitchen. The ground floor was the office of the captain, as well as the quartermaster and regiment sergeants (none of whom were present). Upstairs, the officer quarters were out of bounds to all but the Jarl and higher-ups.

It was noon when the captain entered the barracks. He was accompanied by at least a dozen other men in uniform.

"I want a full report from each division—current supplies, needed supplies, unit counts, everything," said the captain, taking no apparent notice of Pernic or Tagorin. "I want them tomorrow morning. Dismissed." The dozen men quickly filed out of the barracks, leaving just the three of them.

"Pernic," said the captain with a nod.

"Captain Wordon," replied Pernic with a quick nod. The captain wore similar battlements as the other soldiers, but a short cape bearing the Avar family crest was fastened around his neck. His face was sallow and white, his amber eyes startlingly dark beneath his brows. His hair, neatly trimmed and tapered in the back, hinted at its youthful ginger-red amid the streaks of gray around his ears.

"I take it this is the young man the Jarl spoke with me about," said the captain. The captain's voice was slightly raspy.

"Yes, this is Tagorin," said Pernic.

"The Jarl informs me that you have no prior military experience, is that right?"

"Yes," said Tagorin.

"You'll address me as sir, or captain."

"Yes, sorry, sir," replied Tagorin apologetically.

"It's not uncommon for inexperienced men to join our ranks—I'll have you work with the first division sergeant to develop basic swordsmanship and defensive strategies. The sergeant will assess your progress and determine whether you are capable of entering the battlefield. Report here after lunch—eat light."

The captain dismissed them, and Pernic accompanied Tagorin to the kitchens for a quick bite to eat.

"Am I really expected to fight in this battle?" asked Tagorin over lunch.

"The Jarl was clear on the matter, I think," replied Pernic.

"But you could explain the situation," said Tagorin. "I just want to save Dagon. I'm not interested in fighting a war."

"And how do you propose we save your friend, hmm? You realize that Dagon will have long been inside the capital walls of Hoethra—the impenetrable fortress that it is—safe from any attempt to break him out? Tagorin, I've told you many times now that you must be willing to face the king to save your friend. Liberating Aldure is the only course of action before you."

At this, Tagorin could not help but feel discouraged and trapped. Pernic, sensing this, replied:

"You've seen the Avar crest, yes? The motto is: *Courage shall lead the heart true*. Ilandee would spend much of his youth attempting to understand it. Well into his adult life and after serving some time as an ambassador, he confided in me that he still had not found a conclusive answer to its meaning. Ilandee did, however, find a question he felt necessary to get to the answer."

"What was the question?"

"What is worthy of courage?" And with that final answer, Pernic left Tagorin to his thoughts.

Following lunch, Tagorin returned to the barracks, greeted this time by the first-division sergeant.

"I'm Sergeant Bilius." Unlike the captain, Sergeant Bilius appeared to be fit for his position. He was healthier looking and bulkier, and a more intense demeanor lingered in his eyes. Balding at the back of his head, he still retained much of his raven-colored hair.

"Tagorin, sir," replied Tagorin, remembering his encounter with the captain.

"Very good," said Bilius. "Come with me." The sergeant led Tagorin from the barracks all the way through the portcullis gate and into the outer ward. There, hundreds upon hundreds of little white tents were erected without any semblance of order. Soldiers huddled in dissipated masses throughout.

Smithies worked at their grinding stones and forges, the distinctive clash of hammer to iron perpetually ringing through the encampment.

"How many are there?" asked Tagorin, still in close pursuit of the sergeant.

"Four thousand, give or take," said Bilius. "None of them soldiers." This comment struck Tagorin as odd, considering nearly all of them were clad in the same chaffing, rusty leather, and iron as he was.

"Mercenaries, farmers, detractors, idealists, dreamers, and noblemen's sons, but no soldiers," said Bilius, looking over the sprawling force. "The enemy, on the other hand, has thousands upon thousands of soldiers—professional warriors and killers—eager to do their king's bidding. Add to that the rumors of demon knights, real or imagined and it's a lost cause. I'm too old to believe in miracles but that's what we need."

Tagorin followed the sergeant through the camp, zigzagging between various tents toward what appeared to be the center of the outer ward. At the center were various established rings, where recruits gathered around to watch multiple groups of two spar with one another. The sergeant led Tagorin to one of the rings, gesturing that he join the sergeant in the center of it.

Nervous, Tagorin did as instructed. He could feel the gaze of a hundred fixated eyes. A moment later, he was joined by another roughly his same height. The sergeant came between them, holding wooden swords. He handed one to Tagorin, and one to the other.

"Tagorin, I expect you here every morning of

the week," said Bilius. "You will spar in this ring with the other recruits and squires. I will instruct as you go—experience is the best teacher. Begin."

Giving Tagorin no time to prepare or think, the squire charged at him, his wooden sword (though blunted and rounded at the point) aimed directly at his chest as though to thrust straight through. Tagorin narrowly avoided the hit, rolling to the ground in a clumsy fashion, which brought immediate laughter from the crowd. Although he did not bear a full set of armor, his chest piece, the loose bracers, and poorly fashioned paladins were heavy. This did not stop his attacker, however, as the squire quickly turned on his heels and changed direction, charging full force a second time. Tagorin was unable to recover in time from the previous fall, and the squire connected the sword to his backside, slamming him to the ground with immense force. The match had ended.

"Stand up!" shouted Bilius, his tone drastically different from before. Startled, Tagorin pulled himself to his feet, his back pulsating in new pain.

"Hold your blade higher, with both hands," shouted Bilius again, as the squire made the next charge. The squire raised his sword into the air, intending to bring it down full force upon Tagorin's blade.

"Prepare yourself—parry the attack." Tagorin, not knowing what parrying even meant, quickly shifted to the side, stumbling over his bewildered feet. The squire was quick. His blade came down in an instant, striking Tagorin squarely in the chest. Flat on his back and the air knocked out of him, Tagorin found himself in the place he never wanted to be. The sergeant walked up to his crumpled body, his face glaring down upon him.

"Not a damn soldier among you."

That evening, Tagorin slowly and gingerly returned to his room. He made a quiet affair of dinner, again electing to eat in his room. His body ached in ways he had never imagined possible. The armor and leather padding stiff about his body, he removed them one article at a time, each revealing a place of tenderness and bruising on his body. He longed only for his bed.

"Widen your stance, lad," bellowed the sergeant. "And hold your blade firm—it's wavering too much." Sweat poured down the sides of Tagorin's face. He had been sparring for more than an hour with the squire, all while having the sergeant bellowing orders. His body ached; his knees were sore, bruises lined his arms and shins, and his back was stiff under rusted armor and the continued pummeling from the seasoned squire. Tagorin did not think he could go much longer.

He was no soldier. Tagorin felt no more confident with a blade than he had a week ago despite spending nearly four hours daily with the sergeant and whatever squire volunteered. He longed for his bow.

"You won't last more than a scuffle," said the sergeant after the squire landed another blow.

"I'm trying," said Tagorin, leaning his full weight on the blunted sword.

"I'm not sure what the Jarl was thinking when he said he wanted to make you a soldier."

"Neither am I," said Tagorin, more to himself.

In the evening that followed, Tagorin strolled the confines of the castle courtyard, his thoughts heavy. He wondered where Dagon had been taken, and if he was all right. He wondered if the unavoidable clash with the White Riders would lead him to Dagon at all. He hated the trapped feeling of the castle, despite the single upside to his new training regiment: his newfound freedom to walk about the inner ward. Always busy, Tagorin could easily (if only momentarily) distract his mind with the ongoing bustle of the castle.

Throughout the week, he watched as repairs were made to weak sections of the inner-curtain walls and as archery loopholes were reinforced at every guard tower and the two highest turret towers. The inner-portcullis gate was fitted with new reinforced iron, and soldiers and masons alike rushed about to stock freshly constructed murder holes with discarded stone rubble and vats prepped for hot oil. The outer wards were equally under the frantic pace of rebuilding, which Tagorin could observe from one of the guard towers not under repairs.

One night, Pernic made an unusual visit.

"I spoke with the sergeant at dinner this evening," said Pernic. His expression was difficult to read. Tagorin, his body painfully reminding him of the week's ordeal, chose not to respond.

"He says you are not up to the task of battle,"

continued Pernic. "The Jarl is disappointed, to say the least. I confess myself disappointed as well."

"Sorry to disappoint," replied Tagorin. "Looks like I'm no soldier after all."

"And what of Dagon?" asked Pernic. "Is he to be resigned to his fate then?" Tagorin didn't answer.

"Tell me, Tagorin, did you never have any confrontation with the Riders in all your time with Ilandee?"

"We had many," said Tagorin. "It's how we survived."

"And how did you engage them?"

"Dagon and I never had to deal directly with the Riders. We were always with bows, hidden." Pernic nodded. His grim expression slowly turned to one of understanding and victory.

"Tagorin, you are a soldier after all," said Pernic, striding forward to clap him on the shoulders. "You're a bowman. I'll inform the Jarl immediately."

The following morning Tagorin went to meet with the sergeant, as had been the routine, only to discover both Pernic and the Jarl also waiting for him. The sergeant was the first to speak.

"The Jarl has informed me you consider yourself skillful with a bow and has suggested that you join the ranks of my archers rather than waste time and effort on your swordsmanship. I'm inclined to agree with the Jarl, but only on the condition that you demonstrate your prowess before we devote further time or resources in your training."

"Is this agreeable to you, young Tagorin?" asked the Jarl.

"Yes, sir," replied Tagorin.

"Very well," said the Jarl. "Sergeant, lead the way." The sergeant led them from the barracks to an open area between the inner ward and the armory. A dozen targets stood erected at varying distances, with the farthest positioned a hundred yards away.

"Have you ever used a longbow, Tagorin?" asked the sergeant.

"No," said Tagorin. "Only the hunting bow Ilandee had given me." The sergeant nodded, quickly procuring a bow and a quiver of arrows from behind the armory. He handed them to Tagorin and directed him where to stand.

"A long bow is different from a hunting bow," said the sergeant. "It's more difficult to draw to capacity, and it takes considerable time adjusting to. Its range is also considerably longer than a standard bow, as is its accuracy at shorter distances. As you're familiar with a bow, the mechanics are essentially the same. When you're ready, take aim at the targets and let loose some arrows. If you do well enough, I will move you to the archery regiment."

Tagorin took a few arrows from the quiver and stuck them arrowhead first into the ground. Setting aside the quiver, Tagorin pulled the longbow into a ready position, familiarizing himself with its mechanics. As the sergeant had said, the draw was heavier than for a standard bow, but not so much that he couldn't draw it to full capacity. He did have some difficulty, however, bringing the bow down and level during his draw, due to the bow's height. The bow was very nearly as tall as him. After he practiced half a dozen draws with the bow, he took an arrow in hand and readied himself for the first shot.

The arrow was noticeably longer than those Tagorin had been accustomed to as well. Regardless, he decided his first target would be the one closest to him, just over twenty-five yards away. He notched the arrow, took a deep breath, and drew the bow to full capacity. He held his position for a few moments, exhaled, and let loose the arrow. The arrow struck just above center of the target. Pernic gave a short encouraging clap, but the Jarl and sergeant remained silent.

Tagorin took another arrow, notching it the same as he did the first. He aimed for the same target, wanting as much practice with the bow as possible before aiming at a farther target. His second arrow hit lower and to the right of the first, but still distinctly near center of the target. Again Pernic gave him an encouraging clap.

Next, Tagorin aimed for the second target— this one easily fifty yards out. Aiming slightly higher than before, Tagorin released his third arrow. It struck below center of the second target by only a few inches.

Two arrows remained stuck in the ground. His arms could now feel the difference of draw between his standard bow and the longbow. But he knew he had to impress the Jarl and the sergeant if he was to join the archery regiment. His speed considerably slowed, he notched the fourth arrow and took aim again at the second target. Again, Tagorin aimed a bit higher than before and released. The fourth arrow struck just below the center. This time, the sergeant gave an approving nod. The Jarl remained as he was. Pernic was smiling.

Tagorin notched the last of his arrows and took aim at the target farthest away, the one just short of the inner-ward wall, nearly a hundred yards away. Tagorin quickly rehearsed the previous four shots in his mind, attempting to account and adjust for the differences of the longbow. Tagorin exhaled and fired the last arrow. The arrow hit the target, an inch high and to the right of center. This time, Pernic, the Jarl, and the sergeant crossed the shooting range, applauding and cheering as they did, their words lost amid themselves.

"That was skillful archery," said the sergeant. "I'll have you working with the archery regiment first thing in the morning."

"I'll admit, I was rather impressed with your display of skill, young Tagorin," said the Jarl, slapping Tagorin heartily on the back. "Though it would still do you good to handle a sword."

"Yes," said the sergeant. "Even the archery regiment carries swords in the event the walls are breached. You'll need to be able to defend yourself in close combat."

"You will still continue your sparring training with the squires once a week," said the Jarl, turning to leave. However, he turned briefly and said, "I trust you'll be at dinner tonight?"

"Yes, sir," replied Tagorin, overjoyed with the news of his new role.

"Very good," said the Jarl, excusing himself.

"I suggest you return to your room and rest," said Pernic. "Tomorrow the real work begins."

That night, Tagorin relented from his past solitude and joined Pernic for dinner at Enora's table. The tables groaned beneath the weight of the feast. Hams, yams, potatoes, cabbage, corn, and multiple cheeses were scattered throughout the table. Mead arrived by the barrel, and the Jarl greeted him warmly and shared his delight in Tagorin's skill with a bow.

"Who instructed you in archery, young Tagorin?" asked the Jarl.

"Ilandee, sir," said Tagorin. "He would have us practice a few hours a day when we were growing up. At first it was to teach us to hunt."

"It shall serve you well, I suspect," said the Jarl.

Despite Tagorin's newfound sense of purpose, his eyes kept wandering to Enora. As expected, Enora had been adorned with regal robes and dress. She would smile in turns from one diplomat to the next, all shortly lived. And while she had passed him a similar greeting, Tagorin could not help but feel that her expressions were distant and detached. As odd as it was for him, he couldn't help but entertain the wish for the old Enora who had threatened his life in the dark streets of Finoval.

Dinner had ended as suddenly as it had begun, or so it felt to Tagorin. He left for his room, his stomach full and more satisfied than since his arrival. He knew tomorrow would be the first step into a new life—he just wished he knew where it would lead. He wished Ilandee were there to guide him.

CHAPTER SIXTEEN: PREPARE FOR BATTLE

Winter approached Avar Castle as the distant hills were brushed with the first snow. The following weeks passed in a blur to Tagorin, who now spent most of the day with the first division archery regiment. In all, the Jarl's force comprised five divisions, each with an infantry and archery regiment. Tagorin had been placed in the first division, the smallest and responsible for the west side inner ward. His company, one of three, totaled three dozen archers, along with Sergeant Bilius and half a dozen or so pikemen ready to skewer any who tried breaching the walls by ladder. It had been a welcome change to Tagorin. He was good with a bow, and already he had become a favorite among many of the bowman in his division.

Admittedly, Tagorin found the tasks at hand much more demanding than anticipated. Every morning, the division would review countless strategies and realignments given a multitude of situations. They discussed target selection and responsiveness to fallen allies (they were to halve the distance between them and the next archer to maintain the line and fill in the gaps).

Following the briefing, the division spent the remainder of the morning conditioning and exercising their upper-body strength. They would draw their bows to full capacity repeatedly (without arrows) and hold the position in varying lengths of time. Sergeant Bilius kept them at it until noon.

Lunch was always a quick affair. Typically,

lunch arrived as cold slices of the previous night's roasted pig, cheese, a bread roll, and water. They would eat their meal mostly in silence, though Tagorin had found himself regularly amid a small crowd that had something to say about everything.

"I tell you, when this fight's over, I'm gonna make somethin' of myself," said Erik, the man to his right. Tallest in the regiment, Erik had no trouble standing out. Other than Tagorin, Erik was the youngest (as far as Tagorin could tell).

"Don't waste your breath," said Boles, who sat across from them. "You think we're ever leaving this place? Suppose we do win this battle—what then? Our service is done? I don't think so." Boles had one of those deep voices that could penetrate any crowd. His big build, enormous hands, and wide shoulders made Boles the most intimidating of the group.

"Oh, shut it, Boles," replied Demetrius. "A man has to have something to cling to." Demetrius was the last of their little lunch group. He was much older than the rest of them, his neatly trimmed beard nearly as white as the snow of the distant hills. Demetrius and Boles were often at odds.

"All a man needs is a good bow and a sharp knife," said Boles. "Two things in life you can be sure of: You're either living or dead."

"Boles, don't you have a dream?" asked Erik. "You know, somethin' to look forward to?"

"I live one day to the next," said Boles. "You can't plan a man's life in a place like this. Tomorrow isn't always going to come. That's all I'm saying."

"And that's why we're going to fight," said Demetrius.

"Assumin' the sergeant doesn't kill us first," said Erik. They all laughed at this. It had been just before lunch that they had all witnessed the sergeant using the broadside of his sword against the head of an unruly soldier in another division.

"The sergeant has more control over that entire division than its own sergeant," said Demetrius. "I'm surprised he's not been given the post of captain."

"Because the Jarl knows we wouldn't have an army left if he did," said Boles.

"You just don't like being told what to do," said Demetrius.

"You're damn right," said Boles.

After the meal, each division cycled through the archery range every hour. Divisions that were not perfecting their archery skills were given the tasks of retrieving arrows gone astray or fletching new arrows, or they would take turns sparring with one another. Division captains, meanwhile, gathered at the barracks to discuss equipment needs and any other matters requiring attention. For the first time since arriving in Ancleed, Tagorin felt a sense of purpose and couldn't help his burgeoning confidence.

This did not last, however, as the following day the captain stood before all the assembled divisions to report on the recent developments.

"Our resources have concluded that construction of the enemy's ships have been completed, and they are currently on route to Finoval. Multiple supply caravans have since transported various supplies of food and weapons from Hoethra, all in preparation for their siege attempt upon Ancleed. Garrisons of White Riders wait to board those ships. We estimate the king will send a force of at least five thousand strong, which will arrive within the week.

"To date, our forces number approximately four thousand. I will not lie to you — we are considerably outnumbered. Many of you have never seen battle. You've never raised blade or bow to a White Rider, much less any professional soldier. That is our enemy — five thousand highly trained, professional soldiers, armed with the best steel and plate available. But we are not weak. This is our home, and we will fight to the last of our breath to see it free. We have strong walls, and strong wills. They may breach our city, but they will not breach our spirit. You are dismissed."

The captain's address had left them all anything but optimistic. Tagorin knew that like him, they were all contemplating the same thing: did they have a chance?

CHAPTER SEVENTEEN: THE TYRANT KING

The twilight hour was upon Avar Castle when the piercing ring of the chapel bell sounded through the courtyard. Tagorin leaped from his bed and ran to the other side of his room to snatch his bow. Outside the room, the corridor exploded in a mass of noise. Already, the synchronous shouting of "Enemy landed" carried through the castle.

Tagorin hatefully strapped on his arm bracers and chest plate in the darkness of his room. His heart pounded against his chest, and his breathing turned shallow as he peered out the dorm room window. Torches had already blanketed the entirety of the courtyard, bathing it in flickering yet strong light.

The corridor outside his room was in chaos. Soldiers ran from one end to another, shouting orders to each other as well as bystanders. Tagorin found it difficult to navigate what had been in his mind a rather wide hallway. Now it felt cramped and tight as he pushed forward toward the castle entrance hall on the ground floor.

The hall was filled with soldiers. Many were making their way to the courtyard while some made preparations for the castle's defense. Near the center of the hall, Tagorin caught sight of Pernic as he hobbled in and out of the soldier lines.

"Tagorin!" shouted Pernic, waving his staff into the air. Tagorin rushed to meet him.

"Have they really arrived?" asked Tagorin over the noise.

"Yes, they are here," said Pernic. "They are assembling their forces at the outskirts of the city. I shall see you to your post." Tagorin nodded as they made their way to the courtyard.

In the courtyard, Tagorin once again had elbow room, but only just. The infantry regiments assembled into their various formations, while archers darted to their posts along the curtain walls. Tagorin quickly scanned the inner ward for any sign of his regiment. A few minutes later, Tagorin caught sight of Boles.

"That's my regiment," said Tagorin, pointing.

"Very good," said Pernic. He grasped Tagorin by the shoulders. "Keep your surroundings in mind and stick with your men. You're the last line of defense should the enemy breach the outer wards."

"I know that already," said Tagorin.

"Forgive me," said Pernic, his expression quite serious. "It is the way of old people, after all. Be safe. I must return to the Jarl." Tagorin nodded as Pernic dashed once again into the swell of soldiers.

"You should've stayed in bed," said Boles as Tagorin approached.

"Couldn't have if I had wanted to," responded Tagorin. "Both the Queen and the Jarl know where I sleep." Boles laughed. Ahead of them Erik and Demetrius were just starting up the stairs that climbed to the west-side walls of the inner ward. At the base of the stairs, Sergeant Bilius was ushering them onward, his sword drawn and raised in bloodlust.

Within minutes, Tagorin's entire regiment had been positioned along the inner-ward curtain walls. Squires quickly brought armloads of arrows, which were placed in empty barrels behind the wall's merlons. Sandwiched between Boles and Erik, Tagorin mostly overlooked the narrows of the city that skirted the shore and the cold sea beyond. However, turning his head north, he could see the extents of the city and the wave of white gathered at its fringes.

The sight before him was unnerving. He could see the war frigates out at sea and the many dozens of rowboats darting to the shores, carrying as many White Riders as they could allow. Beyond the Riders were what Pernic had called the outer reaches of the Wandering Hills. The fresh layer of glittering snow on the hills beneath the moonlight felt somehow out of place.

Tagorin did not know how long he had stood at his post before the chaotic noise of the castle had fallen to a deathly silence, but quiet it had become. The chapel bell no longer rang, and the blacksmiths had stilled their grinding wheels. Judging from the moon's location, the dawn hours were not far off.

Tagorin knew that once mobilized, the White Rider forces would be upon them in minutes. The city that had only just begun to rise from the ruins of its past would face the threat once more. Despite the newly fortified walls and reinforced steel gates, Tagorin could not ease the deep unsettled feelings at the pit of his stomach.

Tagorin was torn from his private thoughts, however, when a wave of gasps dispersed through the courtyard. Hands pointed to the sky above the assembled White Riders. A massive black cloud began to form, its first shape a slim but expansive shroud that temporarily blanketed the king's forces in total darkness. Then, the mysterious cloud took a second circular shape, pulling its expanse onto itself. Little by little the shape of the cloud changed until it took its final and unmistaken form: a human face. Two blazing blue eyes appeared in the cloud-face as it now gazed down upon the forces below it and the city before it. Without knowing how he knew, Tagorin gazed into the face of the tyrant king: Dedalus.

Tagorin stared into the night sky in disbelief. He had never before witnessed such a spectacle. He had heard stories of magic from time to time gathered around the campfire. Just as the stories of the demon knights Ilandee had told him, he regarded them all as children's tales, nothing to ever consider seriously. But in the moment, he stood speechless.

And then the cloud (or whatever it was) spoke, its gaze directly upon the Avar Castle.

"Triton," said the cloud-face, its eyes brighter than before. Its voice was thunderous and deep, yet very human. "I must commend you for such outright defiance. I am your king; did you not in the days of my father pledge loyalty to the Grand Throne? Surely you are still a man of your word as you were in the days of my father." The cloud-face's words confirmed Tagorin's suspicion. It was King Dedalus. How, Tagorin did not understand. It was well-known that Dedalus never ventured from Hoethra. Dedalus, or Dedalus's image, or whatever it was, turned its gaze once again to the force assembled below him.

"This does not have to come to bloodshed, Triton," said Dedalus. "My forces stand ready at my command, should I choose to have them descend upon the city. I recognize we may have differences, but can we not come to compromise? Surely you, of all the Jarls past, my late father's highly regarded confidant and advisor, can be of great service to Aldure once again. Help me—we need not be enemies.

"Perhaps you believe me to be a tyrant," continued Dedalus, his gaze once more toward the castle. "I think it possible you view me as unfair, corrupt, and power hungry. I admit I have shortcomings; I'm human, as are we all. Have I not kept the law? Have I not continued the traditions of my father and his legacy with the preservation of the White Rider Order? I too believe in peace, Triton. It is only in recent years, with the rumors of your gathering cause, that many of Aldure's inhabitants have slipped into chaos and anarchy. This was not the dream of my father; lay down your sword, Triton. Make the bridge to peace."

"Dawn approaches, upon which time I shall signal my forces to attack. They will show no mercy. They will level all that you have toiled to rebuild. Do not let it be in vain. Send word with your couriers before dawn of your surrender, and I shall spare everyone. If you do not, I shall leave none." The cloud-face lingered for a few moments and then dispersed as quickly as it had come.

The courtyard remained quiet, all within focusing their ears for the sound of the portcullis gate, the gallop of a single horse and rider bearing their salvation. But it never came. They waited minute by minute as the moon crept behind the western horizon and the first pale light of dawn washed over the wandering hills.

At first, all seemed to be at a standstill. The dawn light grew stronger and still, the White Riders remained as they were. That moment lasted an eternity. Then, the war horns blew and the White Riders moved forward in a giant wave, their steps in perfect unison like those of a machine. They were unlike the chaos of the courtyard hours passed; they moved as one body, and it was now that Tagorin began to understand Sergeant Bilius's concern. They were not soldiers. And if his nerves and personal feelings served as any insight, Tagorin suspected they were not the strong-willed men the captain had claimed them to be.

They were afraid.

CHAPTER EIGHTEEN: THE INVASION

Archers, ready!" Tagorin sheathed his first arrow, his hands shaking profusely.

"Get a hold of yourself quick, kid," said Boles. "This is it." Tagorin nodded and swallowed hard, his eyes now focused on the area he was responsible for. This was the moment he had trained for. The first wave of White Riders was already advancing upon the outer wards. Infantry of the fifth, fourth and third divisions stood at the ready at the outer ward gate, their swords and spears raised. The White Riders, approaching the castle, split into two formations, the first (and largest) approached the entrance of the outer ward while the smaller detachment went toward the narrows of the city, the one place where the inner ward served as the only wall between the city and the castle. It was its most vulnerable side.

"Archers, take aim," shouted Sergeant Bilius from the nearby lookout tower. Tagorin drew his bow and took aim at the wave before him.

"Steady." Tagorin could feel the sweat of his brow slide down his cheek.

"On my mark." Tagorin closed his eyes for a moment, once more imagining Lake Gray and the stones skipping across its surface.

"Fire!"

The line loosed their arrows unto the approaching line. A shield deflected Tagorin's first arrow. Few Riders fell in the first volley. Already Tagorin could hear in the distance the battering ram against the wood of the steel-reinforced gate of the outer ward and the first agonizing screams of war.

"Ready," shouted Bilius again, his sword held high in the ready position. Once again Tagorin's regiment notched their next arrows and prepared for a second volley.

"Steady." They drew their bows once more.

"Fire!" The second volley descended upon the Riders, this time their arrows finding multiple targets. Volley after volley, Tagorin and the regiment launched arrows into the ever-advancing Riders.

"Watch the runners," beckoned Bilius. Riders with ladders (two to each ladder) now advanced upon the castle walls. They had prepared for this moment. Tagorin and Boles took aim at the same pair and fell them both. Again and again they fired their arrows upon wave after wave of White Rider.

"Inner ward breached," came the shouts of many. Tagorin turned his eyes from the narrows to the north. Riders were pouring in, and the clash of metal to metal had begun.

"Eyes on the targets," shouted Bilius. Tagorin shook his head and returned his attention to defending the wall. They were no longer firing in unison, as the Riders had spread a considerable distance apart, making it much more difficult to hit their targets. They now focused on the runners.

Tagorin was unaware of how much time had passed, but he knew that it was now into the heart of the morning hours and Dedalus's forces felt no thinner. He knew only one wall remained between him and the enemy. He could hear the battering rams upon the second gate now.

The castle doors were opened then, as some of

the infantry of the first division poured in ready to barricade the castle, followed by the archers, who would slip into the north tower and continue loosing their arrows from above.

"Archers, to the castle." The call came just as the runners had managed to brace their ladders to the walls. Quickly, they abandoned the curtain wall toward the castle while a few pikemen readied their spears for the climbers.

Once inside, Tagorin slipped to the back of his regiment as they ascended toward the northern tower. And it was then that fear fully gripped him. Tagorin bolted from the regiment and raced down the west corridor toward the tower Pernic had told him specifically to avoid, leaving his bow far behind.

The west tower door had surprisingly not been secured in any fashion. It opened easily at his touch. Two sets of stairs lay before him, one climbing to the top and the other undoubtedly descending to the bottom, wherever it may lead. Tagorin quickly made his decision.

Tagorin raced down the spiraling staircase in complete darkness. The clashes of steel and armor grew fainter with every step he made toward the deepest depths of Avar Castle. He could hear the pounding of his heart in the narrow staircase, each pulse louder and more painful than the one preceding it.

Farther and farther the spiraling stairs led him down until the sounds of battle no longer reached his ears. The sound of his feet hitting stone amplified immensely in the deafening silence around him. Still, he pushed onward, his hands against the stone wall his only guide.

Minutes were turned into a thousand eternities as the spiraling stairs went on. He didn't know why he continued down the stairs — the battle overhead was surely more important than anything he would find at the bottom, if he found anything at all. And yet Pernic's words were oddly resonant with him: *The west wing tower is off-limits.* Despite Pernic's warning, he had found in the midst of the battle the west wing tower unguarded and un-locked. It wasn't as if he could fight in this battle anyway — he was only *a boy*, as Enora had been quick to point out. Surely he would be safer and out of everyone's way down in the depths of the castle.

Eventually his thoughts carried him all the way to the bottom of the stairwell. And nothing could have prepared him for what he found. Where the entire tower had been dark and without light, a tall and narrow silver door stood before him, a bril-liant and pulsating white glow bursting from its seams, blinding him with an intensity he had never known in all his life. Tagorin tried to avert his eyes from the glow, but no matter where he looked, the light penetrated everything. The walls and the floor projected the door's radiance, its light reflecting from them like the sun's rays sparkling on the sur-face of Lake Gray.

Squinting his eyes, Tagorin inched toward the door, his arms shielding what light they could. As he drew closer to the door, he could feel warmth emanating from the other side. When Tagorin reached the door, he was surprised to find it very ornate. Unable to look overly long at the door, he could discern only the very familiar shape of the great oak tree design found on his necklace. A second glance at the door revealed that it was without handle or lock of any kind. Tagorin took a deep breath and pushed against the door.

It wouldn't budge.

He pushed again.

It wouldn't budge.

Despite his unsuccessful attempts, Tagorin was now obsessed with the door and its contents. He wanted to know what the mysterious light was, as well as why the door wouldn't open and why it was there in the first place. Over and over he tried to force open the door to no avail. After a dozen or so attempts, he found himself breathing heavily with his back against the solid door. It felt hard against his back, its surface undeniably cold despite the warm air that slipped through the cracks from the other side. It was then with his back against the rigid door that he saw the writing on the wall.

In the pursuit of knowledge
Innocence shall be lost.
The darkness and the light,
The choice to make
Ours alone.

No sooner had Tagorin finished reading the writing on the wall than he felt the coldness of the door fade away. He stood facing the door once more, his arms still shielding his eyes. He gave another push. The door did not move, but instead its surface rippled like that of water. Tagorin pushed again, and a second wave of ripples spread across the door. Tagorin watched as the ripples settled and the door's surface became calm and smooth again. He took his hand and touched the door with his fingertips—or so he had intended. But instead of his fingers pushing against steel or iron, they slipped through the door, sending the widest of ripples yet.

It was the strangest sensation Tagorin had ever experienced. His hand felt as though it were immersed in water but also oddly warm, as if exposed to a midsummer sun. He quickly withdrew his hand and examined it closely, making sure it was still whole and entirely his hand. Being satisfied and convinced his hand was indeed his and unharmed, he plunged it into the door once more. Again, ripples spread on the door surface, fully contained by some invisible barrier. Tagorin took a deep breath and plunged into the door.

Tagorin found himself standing in a large, circular-shaped foyer. The light inside was tolerable but still recognizably the same brilliance that had blinded him moments before. Still, Tagorin could not find the source of the light. It simply existed. The ceiling was raised a considerable height, upon which the most detailed depiction of the dual tree had been painted. From the foyer only a single hallway stretched forward. Tagorin took one quick glance over his shoulder at the silver door and started down the lonely hallway.

It was a narrow hallway, even by normal standards. He had just enough room on each side for his arms. He was sure Ilandee or Pernic would never have been able to make it through. As he continued down the hallway, he began to hear the most peculiar sounds. At one moment, he could have sworn he had heard the chirping of birds, and the next moment the sound of rushing water. Each time Tagorin attempted to focus on the sounds coming from the end of the hallway, they would fade away, returning only when he wasn't listening for them. He continued forward.

The hallway continued to surprise Tagorin. He could feel the unmistakable summer breeze around Lake Gray and the sound of stones skipping on the water's surface. He could hear laughter, birds chirping, and water rushing. All the while he felt an increasingly warm air fill the hallway, beckoning him onward.

CHAPTER NINETEEN: THE STRANGER IN WHITE

Are you all right, son?" Tagorin awoke to the voice as though it had been thunder rousing him from slumber. Tagorin opened his eyes briefly before the most intense light from above blinded him. A sharp pain split across his forehead.

"Easy, son," said the unknown voice again. "The sun is quite bright in this place. Open them slowly." Tagorin did as he was told. As his eyes adjusted to the overwhelming presence of the sun, his surroundings came into focus. He lay in a dried field of brown grass, which he noticed to be very uncomfortable. Then he saw what must have been the source of the mysterious voice that had roused him. The stranger, his back facing Tagorin, wore a simple flowing garment of clean white. And though it was simple and unadorned with any gold trimmings or emblems, Tagorin thought it more elegant than any of those the White Riders fashioned. The stranger's hands were clearly those of a well-aged person, as was the silvery-white hair that fell just past his shoulders. On the stranger's feet were bronze-colored sandals. Without moving his body much, Tagorin scanned the surrounding landscape and discovered he was quite in the middle of nowhere and certainly not where he had been.

"Where am I?"

"You are here," said the stranger. "Where else would you be?"

"How did I get here?" Tagorin's body ached with soreness and exhaustion. The scorching heat of the sun made his head throb and his eyes water.

"You had quite the fall," said the stranger. Tagorin's head throbbed again as he tried to re-member. He remembered the spiraling tower de-scending into the depths of the castle, the growing darkness and the absence of light, and the silver door. And then he remembered the siege upon the castle.

"I have to get back," said Tagorin, making his first attempt to sit up. His body protested under the sudden strain as a wave of sporadic pinpricks of pain shot up the length of his back. Never had he felt so much pain and lack of energy.

"Easy, son," said the stranger. "This heat will consume every bit of you if you are careless."

"But the castle is under attack," said Tagorin. "I have to get back."

"You wish to return to the battle you fled in the first place?" Tagorin felt his heart stop. How could this stranger possibly know about the attack, about the castle, about his fleeing into the tower?

"How do you—"

"You had quite the fall," repeated the stranger.

"How do I get back?"

"I know the way," said the stranger. "But first, let us get out of this heat. There is a garden not far from here where we can escape the sun and you can rest and get your strength back."

"I don't think I can move on my own," said Tagorin.

"I will help you," said the stranger. The stranger turned and knelt beside Tagorin, placing one arm under the nape of his neck and grasping one of Tagorin's hands, lifting him with unbelievable strength. Tagorin opened his eyes to look upon the stranger's face. In the instant following, his eyes grew heavy and he slipped back into unconsciousness.

Tagorin woke this time in the coolness of shade beneath the sprawling branches of a fig tree. The grass beneath him was short but well-tended and soft to his skin while a warm breeze washed over him. Gradually, his senses returned to him. First came his hearing—the rushing of water nearby, the chirping of a dozen birds, and the near-silent beatings of a hummingbird's wings overhead. Then, the aroma of the scented garden carried by the same breeze that had stirred him swept into his nose and forced him to breathe deeply. The aches and soreness of his body had subsided, and he felt warm, light, and rested—new.

Tagorin sat up and leaned against one of the enormous exposed roots of the fig tree. The garden was unlike anything Tagorin had ever seen. Rows upon rows of flowers flowed with the ups and downs of the soil, arranged in a chaotic mess of color yet clearly in their proper place. Betwixt the flowers were rows of short grass for ease of moving among them. Above him was an expansive canopy of fig and cedar trees, all of which appeared to create the garden's perimeter. Beyond, Tagorin could see the harsh fields outside the garden's boundary.

They were brown and dry, scorched beneath the sun.

The stranger however, was nowhere to be found. Cautiously, Tagorin made the attempt to stand on his own, the trunk of the fig tree his brace. He quickly found standing to be easy and set off in search of the stranger.

Tagorin did not know what to call the place. He searched for signs or anything that might tell him where he was or where he was going—but he found nothing. All he could do was follow the paths before him and hope he chose the right one. And yet with all the uncertainty, he knew he would find the place he was to be, though he was at a loss as to explain why. In the end, it didn't matter to Tagorin where he was; only that he was no longer trapped within the walls of Avar Castle. So much had this secret oasis enraptured his mind, he quite forgot that people he knew were fighting for their lives. None of it mattered anymore.

Aside from the fig and cedar trees, Tagorin passed multiple rows of fruit trees, most bearing fruit he had never seen before. Some he recognized—apples, oranges, and pears. He ate one from each, finding them sweeter and juicier than any fruit he had ever eaten. He tried some of the others as well, giving them names of his own choosing. Eventually, his path brought him to a stream's edge. The water, as it had been with the fruit, was startlingly refreshing. In it was something sweet, not overpowering, but just so that the drinker would, given nothing else, be satisfied.

After drinking considerably from the stream, Tagorin decided that following the stream was the right and proper thing to do. And so it was that Tagorin headed upstream. The water flowed at the perfect pace. It did not rumble and thunder, nor was it quiet. Its presence was known, and that was enough. The stream took him deeper into the garden, meandering as it did without any hurry to get where it was going.

Time appeared to have no power in the garden. Hours passed—or so it felt to Tagorin—and still the sun's rays kept light on the garden, its place in the sky the very same as when he had first awoken. There were still no signs of the stranger who had greeted him in the dying field.

It was many hours later when the stream led him to a clearing in the garden. Here a vast field of green pasture lay before Tagorin. At its center was a deep pool of crystalline water from which four streams (one of them the very stream Tagorin had followed) emerged and flowed in the cardinal directions. At the center of the pond was a small island, upon which stood two seemingly identical trees. This was where the garden began; of this Tagorin had no doubt.

As he made his way through the pasture and toward the island, the sun, at first seemingly set in place, began to set as coolness fell over the garden. He then noticed the familiar white figure kneeling down at the pool's edge. As Tagorin drew closer, he noticed the stranger with a gardening spade and a dozen or so bags of various seeds and bulbs. As before, the stranger had his back toward him. Gradually, Tagorin approached the water's edge.

"You are awake," said the stranger as his free hand reached into one of the bags and withdrew a

174

bulb. A space of a few feet in width at the water's edge had been cleared and the dirt exposed. The stranger with the spade in hand dug a small hole a few inches deep and dropped the bulb in it. Then, using both hands, he cupped the free dirt and covered the hole again.

"I don't remember how I got here," said Tagorin.

"You were exhausted," said the stranger. "I carried you here." Tagorin could not believe that the old man before him could have performed such a feat. However, he felt it would have been rude to question the old man.

"Thank you," said Tagorin. The stranger nodded as he dug a second hole not far from the first.

"What are you doing?"

"I thought some flowers would look pleasant next to this pool," said the stranger.

"Is this your place?" asked Tagorin.

"I tend to it," said the stranger as he covered the second bulb.

"What is your name?" asked Tagorin with a sudden curiosity.

"Those in the garden have taken to calling me Keeper," said the stranger with a chuckle. "That name will do fine."

"My name is—"

"Tagorin," said Keeper. Tagorin felt his heart drop and mouth turn dry.

"How do you know my name?" asked Tagorin. Keeper did not answer him but gave a small chuckle and dug another hole. Tagorin continued to stare at the old man. Tagorin had never met this man, and yet Keeper knew his name.

"You said you could show me the way back to the castle," said Tagorin.

"I did, and I can," said Keeper. "But I fear you are not yet ready for what is waiting for you."

"What is waiting for me?"

"A choice," said Keeper.

"What choice?" asked Tagorin. Again, Keeper went silent and dug yet another hole. Frustrated, Tagorin turned his attention away from Keeper and to the trees on the island. As Tagorin had thought, the trees were indiscernible from one another by trunk or leaf. But it was now that he was nearby that Tagorin found different fruit hanging from each. The fruit hanging on the right tree looked similar to an apple but were distinctly larger and clearly not apples. However, it was the tree on the left that caught Tagorin's attention most. On its limbs were fruits of many different kinds and shapes and colors. And yet, among the many, only one fruit allured Tagorin's eyes. The fruit was small, round like an orange, but in all other ways unlike any fruit Tagorin had ever seen. The fruit had an almost glossy look to it—a brilliant and radiant sapphire blue. Tagorin had never wanted anything more than he now wanted the fruit.

"Beautiful, are they not?" asked Keeper. Tagorin peeled his eyes away to find Keeper standing beside him.

"Why are those trees separate from the others?" asked Tagorin, his gaze returning to his fruit.

"Because they have been set apart by the one who keeps them," said Keeper. "Come, follow me." And Tagorin did. Keeper led him around the pool's perimeter to the other side of the island. There a narrow bridge without sides extended the length of the pond. Keeper traversed the bridge first, motioning for Tagorin to follow him. Keeper then walked to the trunk of the first tree that had been on the right earlier and gazed up into the branches. Keeper reached into the branches and pulled one of the fruit from it and handed it to Tagorin.

"You may eat of this tree," said Keeper. "But do not eat of the other."

"Is it bad?"

"Not at all," said Keeper. "Quite the contrary — the fruit is very pleasing and tickles the throat in the most fulfilling way. But it will not fill you. You will hunger for it all the days of your life, and you will not be satisfied." Tagorin nodded; he did not wish to express his confusion to Keeper.

"You do not understand it now," said Keeper, clasping Tagorin's shoulder firmly, "but this you must understand clearly: do not eat of that tree, but only of the fruit I gave you." Then, without any further words, Keeper strolled back across the bridge, leaving Tagorin alone on the island. Tagorin glanced down briefly at the apple (as Tagorin had decided to call it) and then back to Keeper.

"You haven't shown me how to get back," he shouted. Keeper paused in his walk, took his right hand to his mouth, and let loose a whistle so loud that Tagorin was confident it would be heard in all the garden. A small amount of time passed before a brilliant white stallion emerged from the thick of the wood around the garden. Tagorin had never seen a more flawless creature. The horse wore only a simple golden sash around its neck.

"He knows the way," said Keeper. "Until we

meet again, Tagorin." And without another word, Keeper left the grove and disappeared farther into the garden. Tagorin smiled, his eyes darting from the horse to the apple and back again. Still the lure of the forbidden fruit tugged at the edges of his conscious being, but he knew somewhere deep within him Keeper had told him truly. Tagorin brought the apple to his lips and closed his eyes. And then—

"Who is this who trespasses so boldly into what is forbidden?" Tagorin froze at the sound of the sharp voice. The apple fell from his hands, splattering as it hit the ground beneath his feet.

CHAPTER TWENTY: ABADDON

Answer me," said the voice again. "Face me and answer me plainly." Slowly, Tagorin turned about on his heels, facing the direction the voice had called out from. A man stood across the pond, finely dressed and tall in posture leaned slightly forward on a slender cane with both hands resting upon it. He was younger than Keeper, his hair retaining its youthful black. His expression was stern, his lips razor thin, and his breathing purposeful and composed. However, it was beneath the man's narrowing gray-eyed gaze that Tagorin felt an alarming sense of unease.

"I will not inquire of your name again, son. Who is it who trespasses here?"

"Ta—Tagorin, sir," said Tagorin, finding his voice. "Only I haven't trespassed."

"Oh? And how is it then that you found yourself here?"

"An old man brought me here."

"An old man, you say?"

"Yes, sir."

"And who is this old man you refer to?"

"He said his name was Keeper."

"And the fruit you were holding? Took it from the tree, did you?"

"No, sir," said Tagorin. "Keeper took it from the tree and gave it to me." The man shook his head.

"I suppose it cannot be helped," said the man, pulling away from his cane. He walked around the perimeter of the pond, his gaze never leaving

Tagorin. He then proceeded across the bridge, his face as stern as before. It was only when the man was but an arm's length from Tagorin did he speak again.

"The name's Abaddon," said the man, holding out his free hand. It was as sudden as the blink of an eye; the harsh expression lining the man's face had turned to one of cordiality and curiosity. Taken aback, Tagorin took Abaddon's outstretched hand hesitantly. It was then the white stallion that Keeper had summoned reared and whinnied, its head rocking back and forth and nostrils flaring.

"Such an untamed spirit," said Abaddon, giving the horse a quick but disapproving glance.

"Are you the owner?" asked Tagorin, finding his voice again.

"Let us say that I have a...mutual interest," said Abaddon. "Where do you come from?"

"I—nowhere, I guess."

"An orphan, then." Tagorin nodded. Abaddon fixed his eyes on the fruit tree beside him, his free hand just centimeters from grabbing hold and taking one as his own. He paused and a slim smile grew on his face as he returned his gaze to Tagorin.

"The fruit in this garden is superior to any other," he said. "You have been given a very special privilege, Tagorin. Not many can say they have been to this place. Fewer yet have held the fruit you hold now." Then, Abaddon reached into the same tree Keeper had and handed Tagorin a fresh apple.

"What's so special about it?"

"It has secrets," said Abaddon. "Much like the tree beside it."

"Keeper said not to eat from that one," said

Tagorin quickly.

"I suspect he did. Tell me, Tagorin—which of these looks most pleasing to you?" Tagorin immediately pointed to the circular sapphire fruit. Its radiant blue sparkled beneath the sun.

I see," said Abaddon. "And did the old man tell you why?"

"Why what, sir?"

"Abaddon," he corrected. "Did he tell you why you cannot eat the other fruit?"

"Sort of, though I don't really understand it."

"He believes you're unfit," said Abaddon. Tagorin gave him a curious look.

"Both of these trees have remarkable power and, as such, require a remarkable person to claim that power. That is why they are set apart from the others. They are the source. Eating from either of these will change a person forever."

"What sort of change?" asked Tagorin.

"That depends on you," replied Abaddon, "Once you eat of one, you cannot eat of the other. He gave you the fruit you hold now and told you not to eat of the other, correct?" Tagorin nodded.

"You see, when you eat of that fruit, you cannot eat of this one," he said, pointing to the sapphire fruit. "The apple is surely good, but what of the other?" Tagorin shook his head.

"Say a man has two treasures, one of good value and another of higher value. He decides to give one of these treasures to a friend. Which do you suppose he gives, the one of some worth or the one worth much?"

"The one worth some, I suppose," said Tagorin.

"And why not the other?"

"Because it's worth much."

"Precisely," said Abaddon, striking his cane on the ground.

"So the other fruit is better," reasoned Tagorin. He was beginning to understand.

"That is the logical conclusion, is it not?"

"So what will happen if I eat that one instead of this one?" asked Tagorin, looking down at the apple in his hand.

"The apple is good, we know that for sure," said Abaddon. "The old man said so, did he not? And are not all the fruit of the garden good?" Tagorin had to agree. Nothing in the garden was bad.

"And is it not so that a person keeps that which is valuable separate from that which is not?"

Tagorin nodded in agreement. It was all coming together.

"It stands to reason, then, that this fruit is likewise good—better even, as it is separate from the others," continued Abaddon. "Surely, it is not bad. It would not remain were it so." It was then that Tagorin let loose the apple a second time. It bruised as it hit the earth, rolling toward the island edge and dropping with a soft plop into the crystalline pond. The white stallion reared a second time and retreated to the thick of the wood. Tagorin's eyes, however, fixated once more on the brilliant blue skin of the fruit that clung to the lowest branch of the other tree, indifferent that his way back had vanished with the horse. Going back no longer mattered—only the fruit. He had known all along the secret of the forbidden fruit—he had simply allowed himself to be distracted. He knew the fruit to be his; unexplainable as it was, the fruit existed for him and him alone.

Tagorin reached for the fruit, his hands now firmly grasping it. He glanced once to Abaddon, whose face had become distorted by his narrow but widening smile. Tagorin then gave one glance about the garden—they were alone. The noises of the garden had gone soft, and the breeze had stilled. Tagorin gave a gentle tug on the fruit as it separated from the branch effortlessly. His chest pounded and a hunger burned in the depth of his stomach. He brought the fruit to his lips, closed his eyes, and ate.

CHAPTER TWENTY-ONE: THE WHITE ROOM

Never before had Tagorin eaten fruit such as this. All his senses were but a slave to the fruit; its juices filled his mouth and pleased his tongue with unimaginable delight. The aroma penetrated his lungs and nose with such intensity that he could hardly breathe. The softness of the fruit's skin sent warm tingling sensations up the length of his arms and neck. His ears deafened to the sounds of the garden. It was only when the last of the fruit's juices slid down his throat did Tagorin open his eyes.

The garden erupted in sound; the songful chirps of the birds had turned sharp and piercing as they dispersed from every tree. The gentle flowing of the cardinal streams had become churning, tumbling torrents. The warm, welcoming breeze now chilled his every bone. And then, the juice of the forbidden fruit, which had moments ago warmed the depths of his stomach, turned heavy and sour, and the lingering taste on his lips turned bitter. The fruit in his hands decomposed before his eyes, emitting an invisible heat that burned his fingertips. Tagorin begged his body to let go, but the forbidden fruit clung to his hands—it could not be discarded; it sought to consume him. He searched frantically for Abaddon, but he had gone.

The ground beneath his feet began to tremble and quake as the ancient trees fell and uprooted with the shifting soil; the garden was collapsing beneath him. His hands still bound to the forbidden fruit, Tagorin willed his body toward Keeper's tree — the tree that had appeared so ordinary beside its counterpart — somehow knowing its fruit was as Keeper had said: good.

However, Keeper's tree would not be approached; it shook violently as Tagorin stepped forward, its deep roots parting the ground upon which it stood, creating a dividing chasm darker than a starless, moonless night. The ground shifted again; Tagorin lost his footing and fell into the chasm, the forbidden fruit still in his hands.

When Tagorin next awoke, he found himself in complete darkness. But it was an unnatural darkness; an absence of light so complete Tagorin could not see his own feet, much less his surroundings or the hard cold surface he now lay upon. Wherever he was, the air around him was chilled and frosty; he suspected that were he able to see, his breathing would have shape and substance. Aside from the cold and darkness, Tagorin also heard the most peculiar sound — absolute silence. Nothing stirred, nothing moved; all was empty. And yet, there was something unusual about the darkness, something Tagorin could not put into words. He felt safe — invisible.

No sooner had this thought crossed Tagorin's mind than intense, blinding, hot light erupted some distance away, no bigger than a doorway. And though it was a considerable distance, Tagorin could feel its warmth moving over his body. That warmth, comforting as it was, made him feel exposed. And then, in this moment, Tagorin realized the forbidden fruit no longer clung to his hands, but that it must have slipped away during his fall. The bitter taste and the sour and heavy feeling in his stomach lingered, but even so, he hungered for the fruit once more.

Tagorin wondered next how long he had been in the darkness. He wondered how he would ever return to Avar Castle, and if he would ever see Enora again. He knew his chance to rescue Dagon had vanished the moment the brilliant white stallion disappeared into the garden forest. He could not help but feel guilt as well, knowing that he had destroyed the garden over which Keeper had labored so meticulously. And he wondered last of all what had happened to Abaddon (the name made Tagorin feel, if anything, sicklier than the fruit). Then, his wondering turned to anger.

If Keeper had simply been straightforward, then he might not have ever eaten of the forbidden fruit. If Abaddon had not deceived him, the white stallion would not have run away, and Tagorin would have been well out of the garden. Then, his anger focused to Pernic—clearly, he was responsible most of all. If he had told Tagorin the perils of the west-side tower, he would not have fallen into its depths in the first place.

Still, the doorway of light continued to shine, and all the while, Tagorin knew it must be there that he was to go next. Surprisingly, he found that his body appeared unharmed, though he still felt burdened and heavy. He made his way toward the doorway of light, his steps echoing in the dark vastness like those made in monolith halls and marble floors.

When he finally stood in the doorway, he found himself half-bathed in radiant light and half-concealed in the darkness. Unexplainable though it was, he felt rather sure that two forces tugged at him from each side, one beckoning him to the light and the other to recede into the darkness. He moved one step forward into the light, attempting to see what lay beyond the door.

Everything was white and bathed in glowing light. The singular room expanded much like the throne room of Avar Castle, longer than it was wide and braced by immaculate and decorative columns reaching high with no discernible ceiling. Ornate fountains on the right and left of the hallway sprayed gentle spouts of pristine water, capturing the brilliant light of the chamber in immeasurable reflections. Tagorin had never been anywhere so pure.

At the end of the chamber room, Tagorin found what appeared to be a large mirror, easily twice his height and spanning nearly the width of the wall. The most elaborate trim surrounded the mirror, a collection of engraved drawings depicting a series of strange events. Tagorin looked them over briefly, catching moments of Aldure's creation, a great migration from another land, and many wars. So numerous were the depictions that they filled every space of the trim.

It was at the center of the mirror, though, that one depiction caught Tagorin's attention: two trees, identical in shape, and what appeared to be two men and a woman. One of the men and the woman stood together, holding what Tagorin imagined must be fruit. The other man, with a cane, stood nearest the trees. The next scene showed the trees splitting apart from the other, clearly separate. The final scene depicted the man and the woman holding the fruit but cast far away from the trees. Tagorin could feel his heart racing; he had seen the very same trees the man and woman had. He suspected too that he had eaten of the very same tree, and that he too had been banished—exiled. Tagorin paused a moment to gaze upon his reflection in the mirror. What he saw next caused him to leap back and stumble.

The figure in the mirror had not been his reflection at all. For instance, the reflection did not mirror his body but continued to stand unfazed. Dressed in battle garments of black, the faceless figure stood arms crossed, its only distinguishable feature its eyes, cold, faded, and yellow. It was then that the facelessness of the figure began to form and reveal itself as a shroud of blackness dissipated.

In every likeness the figure was him—the same hair, the same nose, and the same chin. Despite the coloration of the reflection's eyes and the faded skin tone, Tagorin saw himself clearly in the mirror.

"Is that how you greet me?" asked the reflection, holding his hands up as though expecting a full embrace. "Although, I suspect it's the first time you've seen me."

"What are you?" asked Tagorin, grasping at the column behind him. The reflection cocked his head to the side as if confused by the question.

"Well, I should think I am you," said the reflection. Tagorin chose not to respond. The reflection shrugged and crossed his arms again.

"Or is it that you are me?" pondered the reflection. "I suppose it doesn't make any difference. I wonder where the rest of us have gone off too."

"The rest of us?" asked Tagorin.

"Well, of course," said the reflection. "Surely you realize that I'm not all of you—yet." It was then the reflection stepped out of the mirror and into the white room. Tagorin felt he could faint at any moment. Aside from battle adornment, the reflection had a long slender sword sheathed at his side, its handle ominously glistening in the brilliant light of the white room.

"It feels good to be out of that mirror," said the reflection. "You have no idea how boring it is in there, looking out into the world through your eyes. And I must say you live a rather pathetic existence." The reflection smiled and kneeled beside Tagorin, looking him straight in the eyes.

"You couldn't save Dagon, could you?" said the reflection, placing a deceivingly comforting hand on Tagorin's shoulder. "And you let poor Ilandee die." Here Tagorin's heart became heavy, and the lingering bitterness of the fruit stung his lips.

"It hurts, I know," said the reflection. "Alone, you were too weak to help them. I can be your strength, Tagorin, if you let me. You and I can save Dagon. You'd like that, wouldn't you?"

"Do not listen to him, Tagorin; he speaks only lies." Another figure had appeared in the mirror.

Unlike the first, Tagorin immediately recognized the second reflection as himself, though it too differed in small ways. This second reflection (like the first) was fully clad in battle armor and had a similarly fashioned sword sheathed at his side, though one major difference separated the two: This one captured the same whiteness as the room.

"How kind of you to join us," said the first, rising to his full height. The second ignored the greeting and stepped out from the mirror, his approach fast and fluid toward Tagorin.

"Tagorin, you must leave this place quickly," said the second. "It is not well for you here."

"I don't understand," said Tagorin. "What is this place, and why do you look like me?"

"Separately, we are Virtue and Vice," responded Virtue, "and yet we are you also."

"He doesn't care about all that," interrupted Vice. "Do you, Tagorin?"

"You awakened us when you ate of the fruit," said Virtue. "Great power resides in us both, but you cannot possess both—you must choose."

"I—I don't know," said Tagorin. He had yet to understand where he was, or why these apparitions had appeared before him.

"We'll make it easy for you," said Vice, drawing his sword at Virtue. "Let's fight for it—the loser goes back to the mirror. What say you, Tagorin?" Without thinking, Tagorin nodded in agreement, anxious for it all to end.

"Very well," said Virtue. "Know this, Tagorin: While separate, we are part of you—our strength augmented by your resolve." Virtue and Vice then, with a curt nod at each other, withdrew back into the mirror, their swords drawn. The mirror had changed too. Once reflecting the spotless white room, it now showed a desolate field somewhere far away. Tagorin then looked inward, a spectator of a battle he didn't understand.

Virtue and Vice began circling one another, their focus entirely upon the foe standing before them.

"Familiar, isn't it?" said Vice. "You and I—this place—fighting for the greater good. You know how this turns out." Virtue remained silent, his grip of his sword tighter still. They continued their slow battle dance, their eyes unblinking and their expressions unreadable. Time itself had slowed to a crawl as Tagorin watched, waiting for the first clash of metal upon metal.

As though on cue by the very thought, blade struck upon blade as Vice charged into Virtue, their swords colliding with force Tagorin had never before witnessed. He could feel the vibrations of the first contact, sending chills down the length of his back. Dust and loose debris flew into the air as they made second contact.

"You can't win," said Vice, swinging at Virtue's torso. Virtue effortlessly dodged the attack, quickly putting distance between them.

"This fight is far from over," replied Virtue. A third time Vice leaped forward, his sword aimed right for Virtue's throat. Virtue deflected the blade and kicked at Vice's unstable footing. Vice then stuck his blade into the ground and launched his full weight as a counterbalance to Virtue's attack, recovering fully. It was unlike any struggle Tagorin had ever seen—their movements born of rhythm and precision rather than the desire for survival. Such was the battle that Tagorin could only marvel at the display of strength as the ferocity and impact of exchanged blows increased with every swing of their blades. And yet matched as they were in strength, Tagorin could also notice how different they were. Vice fought with intensity—his fearless charge into every swing was a risk taken. Virtue, he soon realized, preferred to avoid risk; he fought in a calculated way, utilizing every movement without error. He did not flee from confrontation but stood like a mountain unmovable, deflecting but never advancing.

"Tagorin, you can end this fight at any time," said Virtue as he deflected yet another blow. "Our strength is your will."

"Look at him, Tagorin," shouted Vice, "begging for your help. You think he'll be able to save your friend? It doesn't have to be this way—I can help you. I'll be your strength."

I can be your strength, Tagorin, if you let me. You and I can save Dagon. You'd like that, wouldn't you?

With his blade grasped in both hands and raised high over his head, Vice charged headlong toward Virtue. He brought his sword down as Virtue raised his own to deflect the blow.

A deafening shriek of pierced metal echoed from the mirror. Vice had cut straight through Virtue's blade, cleaving it into two. Virtue did not appear stunned or surprised and immediately withdrew, leaving his broken sword upon the ground. Vice gave his foe not a word of recognition but scoffed and turned his attention instead to Tagorin.

"Bravo," said Vice, "you've made a wise choice." He sheathed his sword and stepped out from the mirror for the second time. The reflection of the mirror returned to that of the white room, leaving Virtue to look out upon them, his expression unreadable.

It was then Tagorin felt the heaviness in his stomach and the bitterness on his lips. His eyes turned sensitive to the brightness of the room, and he longed for the fruit of the garden.

"You need rest," said Vice, kneeling beside him again. "This is weakness leaving your body — you'll see. Soon you won't even feel it anymore and you'll laugh at the days of your weakness. Sleep now and we'll leave this place." Tagorin closed his eyes and slept.

CHAPTER TWENTY-TWO: A PROPOSITION

Well, well, he's awake." Tagorin opened his eyes. Gradually his eyes came into focus and the torch light around him revealed his surroundings. Tiber stood over him, his whiskey breath more than suffocating him. A dozen or so White Riders were in his company. It was now that Tagorin realized he was lying in nearly an inch of water.

"Took a bit of a fall, didn' you?" said Tiber, pulling out a flask and uncorking it.

"How did I get here?"

"Dunno," said Tiber, kneeling down and holding the flask near Tagorin's mouth. "Drink this."

"What is it?"

"Drink," said Tiber, pulling a knife swiftly to Tagorin's throat. Tagorin quickly took a sip of the flask—its contents vile and pungent—and swallowed. A few moments later and his eyes fell heavy once again.

Tagorin woke to his head throbbing. He had been bound with tight cords and laid face up on a dirt floor. Charcoal fumes burned at his nose from the fireplace in the corner adjacent to him. Candles were spread around the room on wall-mounted candleholders, illuminating the small room. There were no windows, leaving Tagorin to think it was a cellar of some kind. The walls were thrown-together brick and mortar. Two stone pillars, evenly spaced in the middle of the room, supported a massive timber beam that ran the length of the room. Between the pillars was a small round wooden table. Stairs leading upward were directly diagonal from him.

Tagorin did not know how long he had been unconscious; all he could remember was being forced at blade point to drink from a flask Tiber had given him. Pernic and Enora were no doubt aware of his disappearance by now and were probably scouring the castle for him. It was useless; they would not find him.

Footsteps above disrupted Tagorin from his thoughts. He could hear men talking but was unable to make out any of the words. He wished he had never left the castle. He was not terribly frightened by Tiber; it was the implications of being captured that frightened Tagorin the most. He had never seen Dedalus, but he feared that meeting more than he had ever feared anything.

Tagorin's thoughts were brushed aside yet again as light flooded the dark cellar room as the door at the top of the stairs swung open. Leading a group of four White Riders, Tiber descended into the cellar, carrying with him a mysterious object wrapped in cloth. Three of the Riders aligned themselves against the far wall while the fourth approached the table with a small metallic stand. Tiber gave the Rider a curt nod. The Rider set the stand on the center of the table and rejoined his comrades on the far wall.

"Finally awake, are ya?" said Tiber, placing the unknown object on the stand. He didn't face Tagorin as he spoke. Tagorin could no longer see what he was doing with the veiled object.

"Where am I?" asked Tagorin.

"Still in Ancleed," replied Tiber. "You've been sleepin' the pas' two days."

"Where is Dagon?"

"Don' worry 'bout that," said Tiber, turning from the table to stare down at Tagorin. "You'll be seein' 'im soon enough." Tagorin winced as another flash of pain seared across his forehead. Tiber laughed.

"Powerful stuff, ain' it?"

"What is it?" asked Tagorin, his eyes strained shut.

"Edna," said Tiber proudly. "Rare stuff tha' is." Tiber then returned his attention to the table. Gently, he removed the cloth, revealing a seemingly solid black globe no bigger than his fist. Tiber then grabbed Tagorin by the sides of his arms and lifted him into a sitting position, propping his back against the wall. Then Tiber did something strange. He walked up to the table and rested his right hand on the black globe and spoke to it.

"Yer Majesty, Tiber speakin'."

Nothing happened. Minutes passed as Tiber continued to stare into the black ball. And then it happened. A cavernous voice filled the small cellar.

"Tiber," said the voice admiringly. "You have contacted me much sooner than I had anticipated. I assume that everything is going smoothly."

"Yes, Yer Majesty," responded Tiber.

"And the boy?"

"I 'ave him," said Tiber. "He's 'ere in the room now."

"Where are your manners, Tiber?" asked Dedalus. "I would much like to have a word with him. He must be quite confused."

"O' course, Yer Majesty," said Tiber. He turned away from the table and unsheathed one of the many knives across his chest. Tiber then proceeded to cut the bindings of Tagorin's feet and hands. Once Tagorin was free, Tiber replaced the knife in its sheath and pulled Tagorin to his feet by the scruff of his shirt, choking Tagorin as he did so.

"Be gentle, Tiber," said Dedalus. "Bring him forward, please." Tiber gave Tagorin a slight push toward the object. The globe was impenetrably black, glistening in its own unnatural light.

"Allow me to make myself more presentable," said Dedalus. The globe turned a dark purple as a black mist expanded within the cellar. Over the next several minutes, the black mist took the shape of a man, slim and tall. Two blazing blue eyes stared at Tagorin.

"Allow me to introduce myself more formally," said the shadow, gesturing grandly at itself. "I am Dedalus, king of all Aldure. I have been waiting some time to speak with you, Tagorin." Tagorin felt his heart leap into his throat.

"Don't be alarmed," said Dedalus. "The figure you see before you is merely a rendition of my true self. You may address me if you like—I ask only that you do it respectfully, as I would do no less for you." Tagorin felt as though all ability to speak had been lost to him.

"You must be wondering why I have gone through all the trouble of seeking your audience," said Dedalus, pacing side to side. "I admit it is unfortunate that my original plans have deviated from their previous course. It was not my intention to deceive you, nor was it my wish that Ilandee's life be taken. I could use his help now more than ever."

"Where is Dagon?" asked Tagorin, keen to change the subject from Ilandee. Not to mention he was in the company of the man he had been raised all his life to hate and fear.

"Oh, I almost forgot," replied Dedalus. "He is here, of course, safe at my palace. He anxiously awaits your arrival. Would you like to speak with him?" Tagorin nodded, unsure if the figure that was Dedalus could see him.

"Very well, I shall send for him." The figure turned to its side, nodded as if he were in the company of others unknown. A minute passed and another figure took shape within the mist. Unlike Dedalus's form, nothing was discernible about the second figure other than shape and size.

"Tagorin?"

"Dagon!" shouted Tagorin. "Is it you?"

"Yeah, it's me," said Dagon. It definitely sounded like Dagon.

"Are you all right? Are you hurt?"

"Relax," said Dagon. "I'm at the king's palace, in Hoethra. Tagorin, you've got to see this place. Everything is wonderful here — more food than you can eat. You'll never be hungry again."

"You see, Tagorin," said Dedalus cutting in, "everything is well with your friend." He nodded to Dagon, and a moment later his figure had dissipated amid the mist. "All that remains is for you to join us here."

"What do you need us for?"

"In truth, I had hoped for Ilandee," said Dedalus. "But now only you two remain. Aldure needs you both, to do what I cannot. I am happy to go over the details when you have arrived in Hoethra."

"I don't trust you," said Tagorin. "I don't know you."

"At least agree to accompany Tiber to the capital," insisted Dedalus. "Hear my proposition in full, and if still you are unconvinced, you and Dagon can leave, free to be on your way. What say you?" Tagorin thought for a moment. He knew Dedalus couldn't be trusted, but he could think of no other way into the palace to rescue Dagon. It was a risk he would have to take.

"All right," said Tagorin, nodding.

"Excellent!"

"I'll come, but that's all I'm promising."

"I expect nothing more," replied Dedalus. "Tiber."

"Yes, milord?"

"You have done well, Tiber," said Dedalus, his electric eyes shifting from Tagorin to Tiber. "While I disapprove of your methods, you have done that which was asked of you, and you shall be rewarded. I have already sent for your transport. They should already be awaiting you." Dedalus returned his gaze to Tagorin. "I humbly await your arrival. May your travel here be safe and swift." Then, in the same fashion as Dedalus had materialized, the figure dissipated and the mist retracted back into the mysterious black globe.

When all the mist had vanished, Tiber replaced

the object within the cloth it had been wrapped in. He then withdrew a pouch from his belt and slid the object inside. Once he attached the pouch to his belt, he turned to the other White Riders.

"All righ' now," Tiber said. "Head outside an' keep the coast clear." One by one the Riders exited the cellar, leaving Tiber and Tagorin alone. Tiber turned to face Tagorin, drawing a knife and pointing it directly at him.

"Now, don' you try anything smart," Tiber said. "Yer still under my watch, an' I won't hesitate to hurt ya. My only job is to get ya to Hoethra. Understand?"

Tagorin nodded. Tiber then pointed to the stairs. Led at knifepoint, Tagorin climbed the stairs and entered the main floor of the house, continuing to the entry, and from there stepped out into the streets of Ancleed for the first time.

It was a ruin of a city; brick and mortar lay crumbled on the streets from leaning and collapsed homes, towers stood with their stairwells exposed, and the streets were littered with busted crates. The flagstone streets that once lay flat and smooth were uneven and missing in large sections, more dirt than stone. And worse still were the inhabitants; they huddled within the crumbling structures, blankets and sheets serving as dividers between them. Children ran in the streets, hardly clothed and without shoes. White Riders patrolled the streets. Tagorin glanced in the direction of Avar Castle; Tagorin could hardly believe his eyes. Both the outer and inner wards had been breached. The north wing tower smoldered from a recent fire, and the portcullis gate had been forced open. They had lost. Enora, Pernic, the Jarl—everyone had undoubtedly been killed or taken prisoner.

"Sir," one of the Riders said, addressing Tiber. "It looks like the transport has not arrived yet."

"Must be slow," Tiber replied. "I'll be sure to report 'em to His Majesty."

"What should we do then, sir?"

"Nothin' much we can do but—" Tiber started but was interrupted by sudden screaming. Tagorin twisted his head and looked in the direction the screams had come from. The sky had turned dark, darker than Tagorin could ever remember seeing during the day. At the far edge of the city, a black mist began to consume the collapsed building, masking it entirely from view. The screams grew louder.

"I don't understand," Tiber shouted. Tagorin turned to face him. Tiber's face had grown gaunt and pale, and his eyes had grown wide. "I've done everythin' asked o' me. He's betrayed me!" Tagorin returned his gaze to the far end of the city and felt his heart drop. Within the mist were green sparkling eyes, and they were coming straight for them.

Run!" Tiber shouted as he lunged past the Riders. The Riders disbursed in panic, running in all directions. Inhabitants fled past them, pushing and shoving each other as they attempted to make their way to the front of the herd. All the while, Tagorin's eyes had not left the far end of the city. Houses already in ruins were falling to the ground in heaps of broken timber as the green eyes plowed straight through them. The black mist melded with blazing tinges of red and yellow as fire sparked to life. The city's screams grew louder and louder, but Tagorin stood still, unable to move.

And then he saw them, emerging from the mist.

Standing almost twice the height of a normal man, they lurched forward, their oppressive black armor glinting strangely in the dim light of the day. They drug the blades of their swords on the ground behind them like mindless servants. When they swung, it was careless and imprecise. Everything the sword scathed fell to their feet. They did not chase their victims, they simply marched forward side by side in a line formation; they were a wall. They were emotionless, their eyes staring only ahead. Soon, Ancleed had become littered with bodies. Given that the knights only marched, Tagorin could not explain how they were able to have made it so far into the city so quickly. In the back of his mind, Ilandee's voice surfaced: *Only those with wickedness in their hearts can see them.* Feeling returned to his legs and he ran.

Tagorin did not look behind him. He ran, uncaring of whom he pushed aside or knocked to the ground; children, women, old men—it didn't matter. All that mattered was living.

As he ran, the story he heard in Zythan was finally complete. He could see everything as it had happened: Dedalus standing at the front of an immortal army, Hoethra falling, the death of Alexander, all of it. These images continued to flash in Tagorin's mind as he ran. The echoes of crashing timber and brick chased relentlessly after him. His ears had grown deaf to Ancleed's screams.

Ahead of him, he could see the head of the crowd nearing a series of white stone pillars, some crumbled and incomplete, others still intact. Remains of arches lie below the pillars. Tagorin assumed it was once the grand entrance of Ancleed. Tagorin chanced a glance behind him. The knights were gaining on them.

Screams rang in front of him this time. Tagorin returned his gaze to the front of the crowd, where the unthinkable had happened again. The same black mist had settled at the entrance as more knights emerged. They were surrounded. Frantic, the crowd burst in every direction, tripping and falling over one another. Alarmed, Tagorin bolted from the main street and into one of the alleys.

The knights were everywhere. In a matter of minutes they had integrated themselves throughout the entire city. The screams no longer came from a single direction but from all around him. It was not long before Tagorin found himself running from his own pursuers. Each street Tagorin ran through, he found himself stepping over countless bodies that lay in the streets. He ran without direction.

Behind him, three knights had joined in chasing him. His body neared the brink of exertion, and his heart struck his chest with painful throbs. Tagorin again darted down another street, desperate to lose the knights. His ploy was as worthless as the others had been; the knights simply crashed through the house on the corner, gaining on him instead of being slowed down. Tagorin found himself at the edge of the city, running along the outer walls. Surprisingly, they had somehow remained intact.

Tagorin's pace began to slow as he turned into another alley. His heart dropped. He had run all the way into a dead end; he was trapped. The knights approached him, and Tagorin got his first close look at them. Their swords were broad and glowed in the same black eeriness as their armor. Their gauntlets melded into spiked couters, their pauldrons thick and bearing the royal insignia Tagorin recognized from the uniforms the White Riders wore. From the skirt, chain mail extended to the crests of their greaves, spiked like their couters. Lastly, from their helms lined like a dragon's neck in spikes, green glowing eyes peered through slit holes of the visor. Tagorin pushed himself against the wall behind him as if willing himself to slip through the brick and mortar.

The knights inched forward, their blades scraping and sparking as they were dragged across the uneven flagstone. Just as Tagorin resigned himself to his fate, he was blinded by light. He felt hands grab both his arms and lift him with unbelievable force. Opening his eyes, he found himself upon a white stallion, held firmly in place by Pernic. Pernic urged the stallion forward as he raised his staff high into the air. The knights had stopped as if contained within some invisible barrier. And then a wave of such magnitude erupted from the staff that it sent the knights flying, forging a wide pathway for them to escape.

"How?" Tagorin asked, looking at Pernic.

"Now is not the time," said Pernic. Again he urged the white stallion forward, and it was only then that Tagorin took notice of the brilliant horse. Around its neck was a golden sash.

CHAPTER TWENTY-THREE: DARKNESS WITHIN

Tagorin did not sleep that night. Hours passed as he stood on the ridge, watching Ancleed burn to the ground for the second time of its existence. The screams that had pierced the night for so long had finally subsided as the mysterious green glow consumed the city. Tagorin knew that no one other than Pernic, Enora, and himself had survived the pillage of the knights.

Pernic had not stood to watch Ancleed fall as Tagorin had. He had built and tended a fire while the screams hit the dead wall of the cliff sides that cast Ancleed into deep shadow, giving the burning city an even greater glow and ferocity in the night sky. Enora also chose not to watch. She sat on the grass with her back to both the fire and Ancleed, her regal dress tattered and torn, silent with her head resting in her hands.

And Tagorin knew nothing would ever be the same. Tiber's betrayal, Dagon's capture, Ilandee's death, and finally Ancleed's final and complete destruction had left Tagorin more alone and confused than he could ever remember being. He looked over to Pernic, who sat rolling a thin branch between his thumb and forefinger as he peered deep into the flames of his procured fire. Anger flooded the pit of his stomach at the sight of Pernic and his calm face. In his last few moments in Ancleed, Tagorin had thought his life had come to an end. Yet somehow, Pernic and Enora had materialized before him in a blinding white light. How they had known his exact position, he did not know. They had grabbed him, and he along with them vanished in a second white light, reappearing on this cliff top. Despite the fact that Pernic and Enora had saved his life, he felt a deep hate for being kept in the dark. And yet, Ilandee had said to trust him—trust the man who hadn't lifted a finger to save Ilandee's life.

"Tagorin," Pernic spoke at last, "you cannot help them by watching." Tagorin pretended not to hear the old man.

"Tagorin, I need to know what happened to you after invasion started," said Pernic again.

"He said he could use Dagon and me," said Tagorin after a bit.

"You spoke with him?" Pernic asked, suddenly wide-eyed. "Dedalus? Was he here in Ancleed?"

"Not really," Tagorin answered. "He used something—some black globe—a shadow spoke to me, like it did when the Riders attacked the castle."

"An Obelix, of course," Pernic muttered to himself. "He told you nothing specific?" Tagorin shook his head.

"I don't understand," Tagorin said. "He seemed so polite. And Dagon was with him. Dagon said he hadn't been hurt at all." Pernic listened without comment. "He told Tiber that he was sending a transport that would take us to Hoethra."

"There you would have been kept," Pernic answered, "safe from any attempts to rescue you as Dagon is now."

"How did you know where to find me?" asked Tagorin.

"Simple," Pernic replied. "I put a spell on you that would allow me to follow you."

"I still don't understand why he would destroy the city if he needed me alive," said Tagorin.

"It is possible that his original plan was to bring you to the capital," said Pernic. "For one reason or another, he must have decided he was better off with you dead."

"What happened to the others?" asked Tagorin.

"When it became clear we could not hold the castle any longer, Triton ordered a full-scale retreat. A full detachment remained behind to delay the Riders so that the rest could escape. Many lives were lost, but so too were many lives saved. They will live to fight another day, and so hope lives on. We knew this was a battle we could not win—it was about sending a message." Tagorin felt as though he might be sick.

"During the retreat, however," continued Pernic, "we were unable to find you. I was even unable to track you for some time—I feared the worst."

"When they first breached the outer wards, I panicked," said Tagorin, distinctly feeling for the first time regret and guilt. He had been weak. Scared.

"Where did you go?" asked Pernic.

"I ran to the west wing tower," replied Tagorin. "It was dark. It kept going down. I thought it was never going to end. And then—"

But he stopped there. Pernic had told him the tower had been off-limits. He dared not say what he witnessed. At any rate, he was unsure if any of it—the garden, Keeper, or Virtue and Vice—had been real. And yet the bitterness of the fruit lingered on his lips still, as did the heaviness in his stomach.

"And then I fell," said Tagorin. "When I woke next, I was bound in some cellar with Tiber."

"I see," said Pernic with a curious look. "That might explain why I could not locate you. That tower descends deep into the underground." They fell into silence then as the fire continued to crackle.

"I have toiled in Dedalus's plans ever since he took power with my creation," said Pernic after more prolonged silence.

"Your creation?" Tagorin asked. "I don't understand. Are you talking about the knights?"

"You could see them?" asked Pernic, surprised. Tagorin nodded. Pernic shook his head. "The creation I refer to is at once more horrific and dangerous than the Knights of Abaddon." Tagorin felt the bottom of his stomach fall. Abaddon had been in the garden. And yet, even as he thought it, he quickly cast the name away. He reassured himself that it had all been a dream. Pernic placed a teapot at the edge of the fire.

"This is not the first time you have heard the name," said Pernic, his gaze fully upon Tagorin. Unable to hide his surprise, Tagorin nodded. He did not know where to begin.

"You found the door, then, in the tower?" asked Pernic.

"Yes," answered Tagorin. "You knew about the door?"

"It is one of many, and you are not the first to find one," said Pernic, disappointment filling each of his words now. "It is why I prohibited anyone from entering the tower in the first place." Tagorin quickly turned his gaze back to fire. Anger swelled in the heaviness of his stomach. In the center of that anger, Vice spoke clearly to him: *You had no choice. Would he rather you died?*

"I had no choice," said Tagorin angrily. "I would have died!" No sooner had the words left his lips did the lingering bitterness of the fruit burn his tongue. And though it hurt immensely, he found it impossible to stop speaking.

"You expect me to trust you," Tagorin said, turning to face Pernic. "You refused to give me answers when I asked. I heard you and Enora talking in Zythan. You've kept me in the dark. And you expect make me trust you? Forget it."

"What did you want me to say, Tagorin?" Pernic replied. "That I am just as responsible if not more so than Dedalus is for the current state of Aldure? That we Sages have brought more turmoil upon Aldure than all the corruption inside man's heart? Such truths are not so simple. And you do not yet know everything." Pernic's words no longer mattered to Tagorin.

"You could have saved them!"

"Perhaps," Pernic said, dropping his head for the first time and speaking to the ground. "I could not assure myself that I could save both you and Dagon. I reasoned that Dagon was safe for the time being, as his capturer's intention was not murder. But you were in immediate danger. I made my decision and acted. I am sorry I could not do more."

"Sorry isn't enough!" Tagorin kicked the ground in frustration. "Ilandee is dead and Dedalus has Dagon." The anger within him grew ever more violent. He felt as though his whole chest might explode. And then it happened: his whole body seized. He could hear Pernic's words, but they were distant. And yet he could clearly hear Vice's softly spoken words.

You do not need him. You were right not to trust him. Ilandee trusted the old man but you saw where that got him, didn't you? Kill him. Kill him and the girl.

Tagorin lunged at Enora, his arms stretched forward as his hands clasped her throat. She struggled but Tagorin was hardly aware. He felt as though he were far away, watching from the outside.

Good, don't stop. She's as guilty as the old man. Even more so: she's the queen.

And then Tagorin saw it: black as the night, an impenetrable shadow cloaked his body. Strength he had never known washed away the weakness of his old body.

I told you I would make you strong.

Then, a blinding white light erupted before him forcing the shadow back to the depth of his stomach, where the heaviness of the fruit remained. He felt drained just as he had in the darkness outside the white room. His consciousness faded.

CHAPTER TWENTY-FOUR: NEW BEGINNINGS

Tagorin woke with the fire still roaring at full strength. He had been laid to rest on a soft bed-roll near enough to the fire that its warmth reached him comfortably. Pernic tended to his tea-pot resting in the hot bed of coals while Enora stood with considerable distance between them. The look upon her face was one Tagorin had not seen before; fear. And then he remembered.

"What happened to me?" asked Tagorin, rolling to his side, his back turned toward the fire while he stared into the darkness of the nearby forest.

"You have become aware," said Pernic.

"Aware of what?"

"Aware of the power that exists in this world, the power that holds sway over man's hearts unlike anything to have ever existed. This force finds the weakness within us and corrupts our thoughts, our words, our actions, and lastly, our hearts. Aldure is sick with corruption. You have awoken, Tagorin, into the great war of our time, the war that is waged in the shadows."

"Is that why I can see them, then, the knights? This corruption—it's inside me?"

"It is," said Pernic. "It exists in everyone. Until now, you have lived unburdened with the knowledge of its existence. You see the knights because the source of their power is the very same force within you that now wages battle for your soul." Tagorin turned again, this time to face Pernic, who had quite abandoned his teapot. He stood over Tagorin, his eyes full of concern.

"I didn't mean to do what I did," said Tagorin suddenly. "I was angry, and the next thing I know I was—"

"It will be alright," said Pernic, kneeling beside him. "No harm was done." Tagorin chanced a single look toward Enora. She did not meet his gaze.

"Will it, you know, happen again?" asked Tagorin.

"It may," said Pernic. "That depends on you."

"How do I stop it?"

"That, I am afraid, is no easy answer," said Pernic. "You must become what does not thrive in this land. You must become pure—destroy the corruption within you—become what you were intended to be."

"I don't understand," said Tagorin.

"You will, in time," said Pernic. "Unfortunately, you do not yet understand the full burden that is about to fall heavily upon your shoulders.

"You and Dagon are no ordinary bandits, Tagorin," said Pernic. "As you know, Ilandee was but one brother of three. As you also know, Ilandee's brother, Naborus, was the Jarl of Ancleed, as Cadmus was Jarl of Zythan."

"Yes, I remember," said Tagorin.

"Understand, Tagorin, what I am about to impart to you is dangerous knowledge."

"I understand," said Tagorin.

"And it will be a burden unlike any you've had before," continued Pernic, with a small sense of urgency rising in his voice. Tagorin nodded.

"Very well," said Pernic. "With pacts of rebellion rising throughout Aldure, primarily in the east, Dedalus is sharply aware that his influence is weakening. Despite the power wielded by his knights and the White Rider Order, what stirs beneath Aldure's citizens is potentially more powerful than either. More importantly, he understands the longevity of his position is reliant upon disunity among those uprisings. He can easily deal with scattered rebellion, as you've now witnessed twice, both here in Ancleed and in Finoval. However, should they unite, should they band together behind one who would lead them, they become far more difficult to engage. This is what Dedalus fears. This is why he feared Ilandee. This is why he fears you and why he fears Dagon."

"I'm not sure I follow," said Tagorin. "Why would he be afraid of us?"

"Because Dagon is the son of Cadmus, and the rightful Jarl of Zythan," said Pernic. "And you, my dear boy, are the son of Naborus—the true Jarl of Ancleed."

"You mean, Ilandee, was our—"

"Your uncle," said Pernic, nodding. "Yes." Instantly, Tagorin found his hand pulling out the necklace Ilandee had given him.

"That necklace came from your mother, Nadua," said Pernic. "She placed it around your neck as a babe the same night she entrusted you to Ilandee's care. Your father had been defeated on the battlefield in a place not far from here, known as the Field of Tears. She, too, died during the onslaught of Ancleed."

Tagorin could see the pieces falling together now; the reason Ilandee could not barter away the necklace—because it too carried the memories of his brother, of Tagorin's father. It explained why Ilandee found the time for something as trivial and childish as skipping stones. And it explained why Ilandee had to chase Dagon, even if it meant his life.

The sinking sensation of immense responsibility twisted in his body as though he might be ripped apart. The revelation that the people of Ancleed were his people and his responsibility left him short of breath and empty in a way he had never experienced.

"Aldure need you, Tagorin," said Pernic, breaking the silence again. "I could not allow you to meet the same fate as Ilandee." Tagorin fell silent, returning his gaze to Ancleed.

"We have to help Dagon," said Tagorin. "We can't just leave him."

"You have just witnessed the kind of power Dedalus has at his command. His eyes are everywhere. We take a great risk even talking here on this cliff top. I've told you once that by committing yourself to helping your friend you will be committing yourself to opposing Dedalus. One cannot be done without the other. Do you still wish to openly confront the king?"

"Yes," said Tagorin. "I will do whatever is necessary.

"'Then I shall help you do so," Pernic said. "However, it is a task that cannot be done directly. Tagorin stared at Pernic, his mind racing. He desired nothing but to see Dagon again. Ilandee's last words still hovered in his mind: *trust him.*

"Yes," Tagorin said again. "I will trust you."

"You are a brave man, Tagorin," Pernic said, a smile breaking over his aged face. It seemed so wrong to Tagorin that anyone could smile after all the events that had taken place. "No less than I would expect from one whose lineage is as noble as the Avar's. Not many people would openly challenge Dedalus."

"What do I have to do?"

"There is much to be done," Pernic said, reclaiming his seat by the fire. He looked over to Enora (whom Tagorin had quite forgotten about) and motioned for her to join him at the fire. Pernic then returned his gaze to Tagorin.

"This creation I spoke of earlier," said Pernic, "was a grand scheme, a fool's dream turned to reality. Its creation brought ruin and destruction to Aldure. We called it The Harmony. It must be destroyed."

"The Harmony?"

"Yes," said Pernic. "To understand it, you must first understand the Old Way."

"The broken tree?"

"Yes," said Pernic. "It is a long story."

Tagorin nodded.

"Very well," said Pernic.

Long ago...

ABOUT THE AUTHOR

Ron Allen Benton is a Montana native, son of Edward Benton and Cynthia Pederson. Ron graduated from the University of Montana with a BA in English and currently holds a Montana state teaching license. He lives in the Flathead Valley with his wife, Beth.